SCHOOLED BY THE SCIENTIST

DRAKE LAMARQUE

GREY KELPIE STUDIO

To Yolande Palpatine, you know what you did.

CHAPTER 1

IN WHICH NATALIA HARROW CONSIDERS HER NEXT MOVE

Naberus and Natalia sat together on the shaded deck previously owned by the governor of St Vincent. Naberus, or Nab as he liked to be known, was tall, uncommonly slim and had a joyous aspect to his features, although his eyes were larger than was strictly normal in a human. Natalia sat across from him, her feet up on a small ottoman. She was a woman of average height, flowing brown hair and possessed of a certain dourness complicated by a determined mania that sparked in her deep grey eyes.

The ritual with the Hale-Harrington annoyance had been interrupted the night before and as the morning wore on, Natalia sighed for the seventeenth time.

"I only wish we had made some progress," she said, which was the first sentence she had said to Nab since she'd woken up.

"Oh, progress was made," Nab said quickly. "Didn't you see the way the boy went into a trance? The way he came back changed?"

She glared at him and spoke acidly. "Yes, I saw how he came back with unearthly magical abilities. My back still aches from where he threw me to the ground. I hardly see how that is an advantage to us."

Nab leaned forward, his hands dangling negligently between his knees and gave her one of his wide smiles, showing off more teeth than a normal human would have. "It is an advantage. His link to the other world, the place of Azathoth, strengthens. The next time you attempt to open the gate the process will be swifter and easier."

Natalia sat back in the wicker chair, her lips pursed. "I didn't consider that."

"And furthermore," Nab said. "He will feel a closer link to the Master itself. There's no telling what such a link may do, he may hear a voice in his head, he may find himself acting recklessly without knowing why he does. He may turn against his friends and come to us for explanation... the possibilities are limitless."

Natalia allowed herself a smile and her shoulders relaxed somewhat. "Well then. You're quite sure of this?"

"Of course, I could scent it on him." Nab mirrored her position, leaning back in the chair. "There's nothing for you to worry about, time is all that stands in your way now."

"In *our* way," she said, with an air of condescension usually heard from royalty. "I should summon the Order, get them all to join us here, we can make this island our stronghold."

"I'm not entirely sure this is the best position," Nab said slowly.

"It wasn't a question up for discussion," Natalia snapped. Her eyes hooded and her shoulders tensed again. "I was stating what I intend to do."

"Indeed, Mistress," Nab said. His smile and cheerful demeanor vanished and he caught her eyes with a peculiar gaze and spoke again, and this time his voice resonated with something otherworldly. "But you will not summon the Order to join us here. You will write to your connections in London, Tortuga and so on, but you will not suggest they come here."

He cleared his throat and his cheerful manner returned.

Natalia smiled softly and nodded to him. "Perhaps, it's better if we stay here on our own for the moment."

"Perhaps it is," Nab nodded.

"I'm so pleased to hear that the Hale-Harrington boy has been corrupted," she said. She picked up the cup of tea she had been neglecting and sipped it. "I feel the universe warming to my cause. Supporting me in my crusade. It feels good, my brother is proud, watching me. I know it."

"I know he is," Nab said.

CHAPTER 2

IN WHICH CEDRIC HAS A CURIOUS
ENCOUNTER

*B*y all rights I ought to have been sleeping. Fucked out and contented by all three of my lovers on the Devil's Whore. Gabriel, otherwise known as Captain Lucifer, had his arm around me, all strong and possessive in a way that sent tingles straight to my dick. I had been resting my cheek on his shoulder, using him as a pillow. Oliver was behind me, nestled against Dante, which, when I turned to look at them, was just the sweetest thing I'd ever seen.

I tried to memorise the look of them together in the dim light, Oliver's golden hair and Dante's night-black locks. It was too perfect, both of them looking serene and content in sleep.

But something had woken me up, and it had slipped out of my mind for a moment, slippery as oil.

My heart hammered as I remembered - someone on deck. Someone who shouldn't have been anywhere near this ship.

I slid out from under Gabriel's arm, smiling as he tried to pull me back in while snoring lightly. I picked up the first pair of trousers I saw and pulled them on, gratified when they turned out to be Oliver's, which were only a little too large for me and had his suspenders still attached. I slipped those over my shoulders and left the cabin, opening and closing the door as soundlessly as I could. All those years sneaking out of lovers' houses in the middle of the night really had paid off in that respect.

My heart was in my throat as I ventured out onto the deck, under the soft moonlight. There, near the prow of the ship, was an unnaturally tall, thin figure. One who I had only seen in the company of Natalia Harrow, who was determined to find and kill me for the purposes of opening a portal between worlds, and bringing through a terrible monster.

Which is an odd goal, if you ask me. Why would you bring something through that was definitely going to kill you?

But well, she does blame me for the death of her brother, so there's revenge involved, but massive civilisation destroying entities doesn't seem like the solution. Perhaps this fellow can shed some light on the whole thing.

Nab, or more accurately, the Crawling Chaos, was facing away from me, his chin tilted up as if he were regarding the stars. I looked around, but there was no sign of any other ships. Ours was alone, anchored in the shelter of a small mountainous island. *But there should be someone on Watch...*

I looked up to the Crow's Nest and saw movement, someone was up there, a spyglass in hand, but they didn't seem to notice Nab.

I cleared my throat, the crew on Watch didn't react.

Nab turned however, and smiled politely, for all the world as if he'd met me on the streets of London after being introduced over tea at a mutual friend's house.

"Cedric," he said, his voice light and soft, but carrying clearly to me all the same. I didn't approach too close, feeling rather more comfortable with a gap between us of several feet.

"I think you go by Nab," I said, trying to sound confident.

He inclined his head. "Nab is fine, or Naberus."

"What the fuck are you doing here?" I saw no point in being coy. He was directly helping my enemies.

5

"I wished to talk." He unclasped his hands from behind his back and took a few steps towards me. His uncommonly long legs ate up the distance, and I flinched but didn't retreat. I didn't want to show weakness. "Cedric, you have tapped into a power you know nothing about."

I rolled my eyes. "Yes, well, my esteemed colleagues have already lectured me on how I shouldn't use it," I said. Thinking back to how Oliver and the others had cautioned me.

"It is terribly dangerous for a mortal such as yourself," he said. But there was a kindness to his tone. "But that doesn't mean you shouldn't try to master it."

"Master it?" My mouth went dry. "I don't understand. Why are you here at all? Is this a trap?"

"No trap." Nab raised his hands, palm out, showing me he wasn't armed. It would have been more comforting if I hadn't seen him use magic before. But then, I had my own magic now.

"Well, what do you want?"

"My... mistress, Natalia Harrow, she wants a lot of things."

I scoffed. "Yes, like my painful death."

"She wants to bring through a being," he said. He opened his mouth, presumably to say the thing's name. I shook my head and held up my hand, more on instinct than anything. That name, spoken aloud, did strange things to me.

"Don't say that name," I said. "I know. And I was under the impression you were helping her."

"I have been bound to her," he said. He dropped his hands to his sides and looked grave. "I have no choice but to assist, however that does not mean her goals are also mine. I have come to you without her knowledge, and if she were to find out, well, it would go hard with me."

"Then why? Why take the risk?" I folded my arms over my chest, fast running out of patience. I wanted to be back in bed with my lovers, and he was talking around the point.

"My goals are different," he said. He widened his eyes significantly.

Oh, so that means he doesn't *want Azathoth to come through to this world? Or he wants it in a different manner... or... No, I don't have enough information.*

"My goals are to stay alive," I said. "And to live my life without the confounded Cult chasing after me and constantly trying to kidnap me. I've been kidnapped quite enough, thank you very much. And I'd like to stay with the original kidnapper." I jerked my thumb towards the Captain's cabin. "Those are my goals, what are yours?"

Nab clasped his hands behind his back and smiled. "I would like to continue to live on this plane without the interference of..." he glanced at the stars again. "I understand little about what happened in the last ritual, but I sensed that somehow you fought?"

"Yeah, I did."

"And although the power itself is of... the Great One, let's use that name. Although the tattoo on your back channels the power of the Great One, you were able to use it to combat the thing, is that correct?"

I swallowed. "Yes, I mean, I have no idea where the power comes from, but I fought it back, I stopped it moving."

"That's very good," Nab said. He moved closer and this time I didn't flinch back. "Your will must be strong enough to wield it, despite the source. That's a very fine thing, very promising. Your sense of self must be very robust."

I licked my lips, trying not to be flattered by his words and failing miserably. "I expect it is."

Nab smiled and seemed as if he'd speak again but then he flinched, twitching as if there was a mosquito buzzing in his ear. "I must go. But I shall return to you, on another night," he said. "We shall continue this talk."

"I, yes, all right." I said. Then he was gone before I could blink. Simply vanished off the deck of the ship.

I swallowed, looked around and then started to yawn as a monstrous tiredness washed over me. I was utterly exhausted, from the ritual and the fight and... well, everything that had happened to me in the last few days. I returned to bed.

When I woke up in the morning I was not at all sure that Nab had been there. It had felt real enough, but then so did the other strange nightmares I'd had over the course of the last few months. And those all took place on the deck of the ship as well. And the things he'd said, he'd been so friendly, so cordial. I couldn't believe the actual Nab would have come to the ship in the middle of the night by some unknowable magic just to praise me.

CHAPTER 3

IN WHICH GABRIEL'S PILLOW TALK HASN'T IMPROVED AND HAS PERHAPS BECOME EVEN WORSE

*O*liver woke with a faint groan, he'd pressed himself tightly against me when I'd got back to bed and now he was pulling away. "Too hot..."

"Bet you say that to all the boys," I managed to mumble, because even mostly asleep my wit is sharp.

"C'mere," Dante murmured, and for a moment I thought he was talking to me, but Oliver sighed happily and I realised he meant Oliver. I felt a wave of something like jealousy, but when I opened my eyes enough to look at them, the jealousy was swallowed by affection and I couldn't help but smile.

Dante was stroking Oliver's hair, and Oliver had pressed himself against Dante's cool vampire skin and the two of them were so incredibly good and perfect and gorgeous I sighed.

"Everyone be quiet," Gabriel said. "Trying to sleep." He turned over and pulled the blanket over his shoulder, and I couldn't stop myself. I pressed my nose into the hair at the back of his neck and kissed him because the joy was bubbling out of me.

Someone's hand found my waist and I was pulled back towards Oliver and Dante, which was a delightful turn of events.

"I like this," I said, to the world in general. "More of this. Let's all sleep together all the time."

"Please stop being cheerful," Gabriel grumbled. He sighed and pushed the blanket off himself again. "It really is stinking *hot*." He flopped onto his back and huffed out another, louder sigh.

"I will not stop being cheerful," I said. "This is wonderful."

"I could gag him for you?" Oliver said, sleepily. Even as a half sleep joke the suggestion sent a thrill through me.

"Don't threaten me with a good time unless you plan to do it." I turned my head to look at Oliver, who was grinning in a not-at-all innocent manner.

"We need to make a plan," Gabriel said.

"About gagging me? Yes, good, let's plan it," I said. Oliver wrapped his hand around my mouth possibly in a pre-emptive strike. I closed my eyes as the hand on my waist tightened as well, I realised from the coolness it must be Dante.

"A plan for what?" Dante asked, his tone mild, as if nothing sexy was happening just inches from him.

"What do we do next, and where do we go?" Gabriel said. "The cult isn't going to stop coming after Cedric, and we made an escape last night far more narrow than I'd have liked."

"Agreed," Oliver said.

"Maybe we should head back to London," Dante said. "See if there aren't some connections we could make use of, get more information on how to take them down? Perhaps even infiltrate their numbers?"

"We're pirates, not spies," Gabriel said, testily.

"You literally have a secret identity," I countered. Or at least, I tried to but Oliver's hand was still over my mouth and holding on quite tightly so it came out rather muffled. He took pity on me and dropped the hand. "You have a secret identity," I said again.

Gabriel was looking at me now, and from the quirk of his mouth he'd found something to be amused about.

"You know, Oliver, I'm more and more pleased that you're aboard this ship every passing day," is what he said. Oliver chuckled and his hand started to snake towards my mouth again. This time I grabbed it before he could gag me again.

"Yes, we're all glad, but the fact is we don't need to do anything too clever or sneaky," I said. "I have magic from the tattoo now, if someone tries to take me I have a way to fight back, whether I'm armed or not."

Gabriel's expression turned serious again. "No, Cedric, I thought we'd been over this last night. No magic."

"It's far too risky." Dante sat up, pulling a pillow behind his back. I rolled onto my back and went up on my elbows to look at him over Oliver.

"It's fine."

"No, it's…" Dante pulled a hand through his hair and shook his head. "Cedric, we don't know what it will do to you, using that power. And I don't want to lose you, and I'm sure neither Oliver nor Gabriel want that either."

"That's right." Oliver stroked his hand over my chest. "Please, Cedric. This is a power we don't understand, and until we do it's better to leave it be. Stay safe, for me?"

Well, that was just underhanded. Oliver looking at me all sweet and kind, without his glasses so I could see every shade of blue and green in his eyes. Telling me he cared about me and then asking me to do something for him. How could I possibly refuse?

And yet, I wanted to. If Nab had been telling the truth, the power was mine to use.

Stalling, I turned back to Gabriel, who had sat up as well, his knees up, tenting the blanket, and his forearms rested on his knees. He was watching me and his eyebrows were drawn together but in a concerned way, rather than an angry one.

"Oliver's asking for himself, but it might as well be for me as well," Gabriel said. "I care about you, Cedric and keeping you safe is one of my highest priorities."

I bit back a snarky retort about not being the highest priority, but I knew it wasn't fair. He had his ship to think about after all.

Dante reached for my hand and squeezed it. "You know I love you, Cedric. I wouldn't suggest you ignore your powers unless it was truly something I believed you need to do."

I sighed, looking between each of them and seeing concern, affection and above all sincerity from all three.

"All right, fine." I held my hands up in surrender. "But only because you're all being uncommonly sweet."

Oliver kissed my cheek and Gabriel smiled and my heart did a funny fluttery thing and I found I couldn't look any of them in the eye. Warmth flooded me, and my fingertips tingled, I was so pleased. It was so lovely of them all to say they cared.

"So, we didn't get anywhere with a plan for what's next," Oliver said, I presume to Gabriel.

"Well, there was something about gags," I mumbled.

"Absolutely insatiable." Oliver bit my shoulder, his tone one of mock-surprise.

"Which really shouldn't be a surprise for you," I said, managing to raise my chin enough to look at his face if not directly into his eyes.

"Come on, we ought to start the day," Gabriel said. "The gags can come later, tonight perhaps."

I groaned. "You are such a tease."

CHAPTER 4

IN WHICH THE THREAT OF A GOOD TIME IS FULFILLED

After dinner that night Gabriel and Dante got into a deep conversation about whether or not it was going to storm and if they needed to adjust the planned course of the Devil's Whore. I had been enjoying a nice glass of red wine and chatting with Marco when Oliver sat himself beside me.

"Hello," I said, half turning to smile at Oliver.

"I'm terribly sorry, Marco," Oliver said, leaning a little past me. "But I have to take Cedric this instant, we had a particular plan..."

I had all but forgotten the pillow talk of that morning, but when Oliver said that it all came back and my cock half hardened.

Marco grinned. "Of course, I wouldn't dream of getting in between you two. Unless you really wanted me too." He winked at me flirtatiously and I grinned, grabbing Oliver's hand.

"I don't mind if you don't, Ollie."

"Maybe another time," Oliver said. He stood and yanked me to my feet and together we hurried to his cabin. Knowing he was likely to make good on his threats I thought I might as well make it worth his while.

"So insistent, Oliver. It's just not like you," I said. "Like something's got under your skin. I wonder what it could have been."

"Stop being cute," Oliver said. It had the tone of a command but he was still sort of laughing so I pulled my hand away from his. He shut the door to his cabin behind us.

"I can't stop being cute," I said. "It's just who I am. I can't change my face, I can't change my voice, I can't change my cute nature."

Oliver was on me in a moment, pushing me back against his cabin door and grinding a leg between mine. I groaned instead of continuing to needle him.

"I'm going to gag that beautiful mouth of yours and get a few seconds of peace," he growled, then kissed me so hard I practically forgot my name.

My hands were pulling his vest and shirt open and pushing them back off his shoulders, and my fingers caressed his skin, warm and smooth. He did the same to me, pulling my shirt open and pulling me to him by my waist, his fingers then moving to undo my trousers and I happily stepped out of them as they fell.

I couldn't quite be close enough, and I longed for him to pull me still closer to him although there was barely a hair between us. "Oh, Oliver."

He pulled back and guided me to the bed with his hands on my waist. "Get up there."

Because it was Oliver, adorable, over-organised and prepared Oliver, there were supplies on the bed already. A soft looking red cotton scarf, of the kind sailors wear around their necks, and a coiled hank of red rope he must've borrowed from Gabriel. I felt my face flush hot and tried to catch my breath. I got onto the bed and touched the rope, smiling at the smooth feel of it.

"That's for me to play with, not you," Oliver said. He was ridding himself of his trousers.

"Well, if you truly intend to gag me," I said, slowly. "Let me tell you now that the golden glow of your skin drives me to distraction and I am grateful every time you stick your dick in me."

"For goodness's sake," Oliver rolled his eyes but he was smiling and he was trying not to be affectionate about it, I could tell.

"And you won't be able to make any use of my mouth in more enjoyable ways, if you gag me." I wasn't truly trying to talk him out of it, just tease him so that he'd be more strict with me, perhaps.

He was on me again, pushing me further up the bed. When he was happy with my position in the center of the bed he broke the kiss. "You can choose if you're on your back, your front or kneeling, Cedric. Then I'll gag you. Tell me though, if you want me to stop while you can't speak, how will you signal it?"

I swallowed a quip and considered. "I could snap my fingers." I demonstrated the noise. Oliver nodded.

"Yes, that's very good. Now, what position?"

That was a much harder question. I pondered. "Knees, I think, then I can see more of you."

Oliver grinned and picked up the red scarf, carefully folded it then tied a knot in the centre. "This will go behind your teeth," he said. "Open up."

I bit my lower lip. I was rock hard and wanting him to do this so badly, but a bratty instinct flared up in me. I gave him a grin.

"Cedric." Oliver moved closer and brought the gag to my mouth. "Open, or I'll pinch your nose until you have to and that won't be nearly as sexy."

"Fine," I replied. The moment I opened my mouth he had pushed the knotted fabric inside my mouth and was tying the scarf at the back of my head. my teeth came down on the knot and it fitted quite snugly behind my teeth. I found myself tonguing it, curious at this new thing in my mouth. Oliver knotted it tightly, so it couldn't move.

"How's it feel?"

"uhhh?" I wasn't at all sure I'd be able to speak. Oliver's eyes twinkled.

"What was that, pet? I didn't quite hear your answer. Speak up."

"Mmph mmph." I'd meant to say 'ha ha' in a cuttingly sarcastic manner but the gag ate it up. I resolved not to try to speak any more.

"Lovely." Oliver leaned in and kissed my lips over the gag. It was rather arousing, especially since I couldn't kiss back the way I wanted to.

He broke the kiss to take my wrists, pull them behind my back and tightly bind them, then wound the rope up to my elbows and then across my chest, making short work of binding me securely. I moaned into the gag and he grinned.

"Now I have you where I want you," he murmured, his voice more of a purr than normal. "Whatever shall I do with you now?"

I moved closer to him, shuffling on my knees, and he leaned in to kiss my neck. It made my toes curl and my breath catch and I wanted to moan my appreciation so I did, I moaned into the gag and was rewarded when Oliver's mouth moved down and sucked on one of my nipples.

So he wanted to hear me make noise? I could make noise.

I moaned louder as Oliver transferred his attention to my other nipple and his hand closed around my cock and started to stroke. I didn't need the attention there, I was already rock hard from my beloved Oliver taking control of me, but it felt divine.

"I should have done this ages ago," he murmured, kissing his way back up my chest. He caught his breath and looked me in the eye and the pure lust I saw there nearly finished me. "When you were whining your way through Latin or complaining you didn't need to know what dates the kings and queens reigned for. Can you imagine? If I'd tied you to a chair and gagged you during those classes?"

Could I imagine it? I had been imagining it at the time, I'd just never imagined he'd go for it.

I nodded my head.

"You *can* imagine it? Hah. Maybe I'll tie you to a chair next time we're on land, get a cane out..."

I groaned, hoping it sounded like a yes.

Maybe his intention is to make me orgasm with his words and his hand, it wouldn't be hard if he keeps on like this.

"You were so infuriating then, it makes it all the more satisfactory now that I can do this to you, work out my desires on you."

I nodded again, trying to encourage him. He let go of my cock and moved behind me, spanking me hard with the flat of his palm so that I cried out. The noise muffled but still distinct, he spanked me again and I groaned, feeling my eyes close and my body shudder with need, but also with the need to be good and do what he wanted. I would stay still on my knees and take his punishment if that's what he wanted me to do.

I let my head fall forward a little, hoping I looked more contrite. "Very good, Cedric," he said. He rubbed his hand over my arse and then parted the cheeks, his fingers probing at me. "Do you want me inside you?"

I nodded again and he chuckled. "Say yes, I want to hear it."

I tried, but the gag made it sound barely like a word. Oliver laughed louder, genuinely delighted from the sound of it. "Good boy."

He stretched me slowly, which would have been frustrating, only he praised me throughout, telling me I was doing well and being good and I felt myself relax into a blissed out state of happiness. I wasn't impatient, I knew Oliver would give me what I needed, I trusted him. And besides, what else could I do? I was bound and gagged at his whim.

When he pushed into me I groaned with joy. He filled me slowly, taking his time with this as well, and grunting softly, although if it was from the effort of being so controlled about it or the desire he had for me I wasn't sure.

I leaned my back against his chest as he wrapped his arm around my waist and his other hand began to pump my cock again. "You like that, Cedric?"

"Mmmm." I rested my head on his shoulder and nodded, feeling his cheek against my temple.

"So do I, you're so handsome you know." He went back into praising me and I closed my eyes once more. I rocked my hips back as he pushed forward and felt him fill me utterly. "Always want you so much."

It didn't take long, between his murmuring compliments to me and the rock and pull of his hips before I was close and he was panting in my ear.

"Come for me Ced, let me feel how good it is for you, let me feel how aroused you are by my treatment of you."

I didn't need more provoking than that. I straightened up and came with a buck of the hips, shoving myself into his hand and then back onto him and moaning into the gag.

"Oh fuck." Oliver filled me with another thrust and I felt him press his forehead to the back of my neck. We stayed like that for a moment, me up on my knees and panting, and him with his arms around me and his face pressed against me, both of us trying to catch our breath.

"Just want to keep you like this and do it all again," he breathed.

I nodded slowly, trying to form words he could understand around the gag. Then I felt his hands move back, undoing the ropes and freeing me, finally undoing the knot at the back of my head and pulling the gag gently out.

"You could," I said, my voice a little hoarse. "Keep me."

Oliver lay down, pulling me on top of him. "I'm not sure that any of us can truly keep you, Ced, but that's all right. I have you for now."

He kissed me and I ignored the wave of sadness that threatened from his words. I didn't need to think about the future now, all I needed to do was stay here with Oliver.

I snuggled into his neck and pulled him closer against me.

"You did so very well," he said. "Did you like the gag?"

"*Yes.*"

"Excellent. It rather suited you," he said. "We'll play with it again, soon."

CHAPTER 5

IN WHICH CEDRIC CALLS GABRIEL A PEACH AND THERE ARE NO REPERCUSSIONS

A day later in the early afternoon, I was partway through a painting. It was of Oliver and Dante sleeping together, painted from memory because even I knew better than to ask them to pose for it, when there was a call from the crow's nest.

I was painting on an easel just inside the door of the Captain's Cabin, because the way the light fell through the leaded windows was very pretty. I left the door open so I could feel involved in the workings of the crew as I painted. And by workings, I mean I could watch Oliver, Dante and Gabriel as they did their everyday things and imagine them naked. It was rather distracting from the painting, but very enjoyable.

The call distracted me from my work on Oliver's eyelashes, and I stuck my paintbrush behind my ear and went just outside the door to hear better.

"Looks like a merchantman, heavy in the water," Marco called from the top of the mast. "Don't see any guard ships! What do you say, Captain?"

All eyes went to Gabriel, who was tapping his finger on his chin as he considered. "Let's take it, we're headed for Tortuga, we can sell whatever we like there. All hands on deck!"

The deck became a swarm of activity as the crew of the

Devil's Whore got to their stations and began to prep for battle. The ship swung around, heading towards the merchantman in the distance. It did look like it was sailing low in the water, which was good news for us, the Whore was built for speed and could cut across the waves far faster.

I set my painting things down and pulled on a shirt, before taking down Gabriel's impressive black Captain Lucifer coat and laying it over my arm. I carried it up to him.

He was at the helm with Bilal. "Thank you, Cedric." He took the coat off me and shrugged it on, instantly looking far more impressive and frightening. I wasn't sure if he actually stood up straighter when he had the coat on or if it was just an illusion, but he looked bigger.

"Captain Lucifer," I breathed, hardly aware of all the arousal I channeled into those words until they were out of my mouth.

Hearing me, he gave me a wink and a smile full of wickedness. "Now, you get below deck, puppy."

My eyes widened. "Wait, no, you don't have to stash me below, I can fight back, I can help the gunners, I can do something!"

Gabriel frowned at me and narrowed his eyes. Perhaps he was weighing up the amount of pouting I'd do if he stuck to the order. I did a quick mental tally of the likelihood myself and it was astoundingly high.

"Listen, I just want to see what it's like, I'll stay back if you like, just... please don't make me wait and wonder and hear all the sounds and not know who's been stabbed?"

He sighed heavily and put his hand on my shoulder. "All right. You can stay up here, by the helm with Bilal. But stay up here, and don't do anything foolish, or I swear by the sea I'll whip your hide raw."

I bit back my glee in order to deliver the next quip with the gravitas it deserved. "I must once again ask you not to threaten me with a good time."

"I regret it already," Gabriel huffed.

"I'll be good," I said quickly. Because I knew and Gabriel knew that if he ordered me again I'd do it.

Hell, if he ordered me to go chain myself to his bed, I'd do it. And lie there getting all hot and bothered while they attacked a ship and hope that he'd come in and ream me. Like he did that first time...

"Whatever you're thinking..." Gabriel said. I realised I'd closed my eyes as I got lost in my little daydream. "Stop. Keep your wits about you. And tell me about it later, we'll see if we can't make it come true."

"You're a peach." I went up on my tiptoes and kissed him. "Be careful, won't you?"

Gabriel kissed me back and then nodded gruffly. "Always am."

CHAPTER 6

IN WHICH THE DEVIL'S WHORE ENGAGES
A SHIP

*E*ven with his oh so manly assertion that he was always careful, I couldn't quell the fear I felt from watching my lovers Gabriel, Dante, and Oliver arm themselves and head into battle. Part of me was surprised at Oliver's apparent willingness to join the piracy, but then a few of my assumptions about him had been entirely wrong so perhaps it wasn't such a surprise.

The merchant ship, which appeared to be called The Green Knight, had raised a white flag. Perhaps they recognised our ship, or perhaps they simply hadn't expected to be attacked. It didn't seem like a very clever or sustainable way to run a shipping operation, which seemed a little suspicious.

"Is it common for a ship to be out without any guards or defence?" I asked Bilal.

They shook their head. "No, there's usually a guard ship, or cannons on board. Either the captain's a coward, not paid enough to defend the ship or just plain stupid. Or perhaps they're hoping we'll spare their lives if they don't fight back."

"Hm." I folded my arms. "It could be the cult..."

"Could well be," Bilal said. Their hands were on the helm, steering us expertly alongside the merchant ship. Marco, Kaito and the others threw ropes over, securing the two ships together.

Gabriel led the charge over to the merchant ship and immediately came the clashing of steel. The crew of The Green Knight had been hiding, waiting for the moment the pirates boarded to attack.

"Ah," Bilal said, as if this wasn't entirely surprising. "Perhaps they cannot man the cannons, or they're not in working order. They thought they could repel us hand to hand." They shook their head. "Idiots."

I swallowed, watching as the battle raged over the decks of The Green Knight.

Gabriel, impressive and standing a half head over everyone else, his sword coming down with deadly precision.

Dante used his vampiric speed to excellent advantage. He slipped under the guard of the man he was fighting and stabbed him at close range, then twisted away to grip another man by the neck as he slashed at Oliver.

Oliver was engaged in battle, which, honestly, I'd never get sick of watching. All three of my lovers were devastatingly gorgeous and arousing in battle. He used his strength to wield one of Gabriel's cutlasses two handed.

Scratch was fighting nearby and watching Oliver's back, for which I was very grateful indeed.

I moved a little closer, down off the top deck, since it appeared the pirates were making characteristically short work of their enemies and I wanted to see.

There was a yell, someone desperate, a slim knife in each hand ducked under Marco's guard onto the Devil's Whore, presumably in a last bid for freedom. Unfortunately I'd moved right into his path and he vaulted over the ship's railings and landed directly before me. He stabbed at me with one of the stilettos. I backed up quickly, raised my hand and sent a blast of magic into the end of his weapon.

The thing glowed red hot and he cried out again, much louder this time, and dropped his knife, looking at his hand and swearing as he shook it out. There was more building inside me, and I realised I could do more.

I felt the thrill of power through my veins. Threads of heat flared on my back but in a way that didn't burn, rather sent energy into me. I raised my hand palm out and shot pure light at the man, blasting him back onto the deck.

Bilal stepped past me and ran him through with their sword. "Nice teamwork," Bilal said, looking back at me.

"Thanks." I looked over at the ship to see Gabriel looking back at me and my stomach sank. I'd promised not to use it and then, at the first opportunity what did I do?

Blasted the guy who was going to stab me, and saved my life, most probably. Bilal needed time to get down here.

But my stomach didn't feel any better at all. I swallowed.

Gabriel turned away to yell orders to the crew as the last few defenders of the Green Knight went to their knees and put their hands behind their heads.

CHAPTER 7

IN WHICH CEDRIC RELATES A STORY TO OLIVER AT GABRIEL'S REQUEST

Shortly after the battle, Gabriel, Dante, Oliver and I met in the Captain's Cabin. Gabriel sat on his bed, Oliver leaned against the desk, Dante stood stiffly on the other side of the room. I gravitated towards Oliver.

"Cedric, I'm absolutely furious that you used the magic of the tattoo," Dante said. He folded his arms over his chest. "Especially after you agreed not to."

"Well, I'd hope you'd be happy that I didn't just stand there and let him run me through," I said. I raised an eyebrow at him and he looked away.

"I'm glad about that," Oliver said. He ruffled my hair with his hand.

"And you might notice that there's been no sudden influx of Cultists or sea monsters, so whatever affect my magic has had, it hasn't brought any more danger upon us."

Gabriel had been frowning but he shrugged a shoulder. "That is a good point. We don't know, however, if it might have alerted Natalia Harrow or her weird servant to our whereabouts."

"Well..." I hadn't considered that. "Well, they don't have a boat, so far as we know, so it shouldn't matter too much."

Gabriel and Dante exchanged looks and for a moment I thought they were going to leave the room and have a heated discussion the way they used to. Would they invite Oliver to go with them? I moved closer to him and took his hand in a preemptive bid to not be excluded.

But they seemed to have an understanding purely from looking at each other because Dante dropped his hands to his sides.

"It's fine," Gabriel said. "This time. If you're under direct threat, it makes sense to use whatever weapon you have to hand. But don't go frivolously using it whenever or wherever you like."

I nodded, relieved. "Yes, makes sense. Very good, Captain."

Dante huffed, looked at the Captain and then at me, and stalked out of the cabin without a word, slamming the door behind him. My stomach dropped away.

Oliver took my hand and pulled me to him. "It's all right," he said. "He's just worried about you, we all are."

"Indeed." Gabriel sighed. "That's rather killed my mood though."

"Your mood?" Oliver said, looking at Gabriel over my shoulder.

"Yes, I often feel my blood is up after a fight," Gabriel said. "And after a victory as concise as this one, I like to work off that energy in a satisfying way, if there is a willing body around, of course."

I swallowed down the bad feeling I had after Dante had left. I set my worry for him aside, my concerns about what he thought about me and concentrated on what I knew I was good at.

Emptying my mind, somewhat, I rocked my hips against Oliver's, teasing him. "A willing body?" I asked, rather innocently.

Oliver chuckled and pulled away, looking at Gabriel. "How killed is your mood, did you say?"

Gabriel leaned back on his hands and looked at the two of us, considering. I licked my lips and decided to sway his opinion. "You did look incredibly impressive out there, Captain."

"Did I?" Gabriel drawled the question out, tempting me to praise him some more perhaps?

Well, when have I ever resisted temptation?

"Yes, tall and handsome," I said, moving towards him, making sure to sway my hips. "Striking fear into the hearts of all your enemies, and awe into mine." I may have been laying it on slightly thick, but it was all true. Every time I thought I'd got used to how tall and gorgeous the Captain was, I'd look at him again, really see him, and my breath would catch in my throat. It made my heart speed up and I wanted more than anything else to give myself to him.

He smirked, reaching a hand out as if to draw me in. I took it slowly, pretending for a moment I was a shy lady at a ball. "Do you remember the first time I asked you to fuck me?" I asked, softly.

He pulled me into his lap. "Indeed, have you told Oliver that story?"

"Not in so many words," Oliver said. I straddled Gabriel's lap and swallowed at how hot the memory of it made me even now. Gabriel, the scoundrel that he was, must have picked up on my meaning without asking, and decided to torture me by palming me through my trousers.

"Perhaps you should paint him a picture, with your words," Gabriel said. I whined, softly, wanting more of the touch. He clicked his tongue. "You brought it up, puppy. You tell him."

"I woke up all tied up," I said, tipping my head back. Oliver had moved in behind me, pressing his thighs to Gabriel's knees and stroking his hands over my body, removing my shirt. I lifted my arms obligingly so he could pull it over my head.

"All tied up?"

"Securely, very very tight," I said. I rocked my hips to rub myself against Gabriel's hand. "And I think that was Dante's handiwork."

For a moment I felt a pang that Dante wasn't joining us, but Oliver's mouth on my shoulder distracted me.

"It was. I told him to ensure you couldn't move so much as a finger, we had to put fear into you, after all."

Oliver laughed low, leaned over my shoulder to kiss Gabriel's jawline softly. "Let me guess, there wasn't as much fear as you'd have liked."

"There was not."

"I was a bit afraid," I protested. I reached up to the back of Oliver's head and pulled him in to kiss me. "Until I saw how handsome he was."

"He is very, very handsome," Oliver murmured. With my hand still on the back of Oliver's neck I directed him closer to Gabriel and moaned softly as they kissed within inches of my own mouth.

"He was gagged too, just at first," Gabriel said.

"Again, teasing me with a gag."

"I'd like to see Cedric like that," Oliver said. "Maybe we should recreate the circumstances some time?"

"Fuck yes."

"He said 'do me'," Gabriel said. "He said I might have to remove his trousers for him."

Oliver laughed, slipped his arms around me and started undoing my trousers. Gabriels hands stroked over my chest and I felt myself getting goose pimples. There was nothing as brilliant as being with these two and Dante, of course, but being sandwiched between Gabriel and Oliver was a close runner up to the best thing that had ever happened to me.

I busied myself pulling Gabriel's black shirt open and pushing it off his shoulders.

Oliver's hands fell away and I slipped off Gabriel's lap so I could rid myself of my trousers, and then help Oliver's with his.

Gabriel stripped without getting off the bed, and moved backwards, getting into the center of the mattress and going to his knees.

Oliver kissed me hard once we were both naked, and I moaned into his mouth, pressing close against him.

"Go on," he said, when the kiss was done. "Go ask the Captain like you did that first time."

"He didn't so much ask as demand," Gabriel said. I wiggled my arse at Oliver as I climbed up on the bed and crawled between Gabriel's legs.

"Please, Captain, won't you please do me?" I licked my lips and ran my hands up the insides of his thighs.

Gabriel groaned and pulled me on top of him, kissing me hard. Oliver was close behind again, I felt the mattress shift as he got on, and his hands on my hips and then pulling my arse cheeks open.

I rolled my hips, trying to somehow make it easier for him, when I felt his nose and then his tongue, quick and slick teasing at me.

"Oh for the love of..." I stuttered against Gabriel's skin, forgetting entirely what I was doing with him, lost in the sensations Oliver was giving me.

Gabriel's dark chuckle sent another thrill through me, and he took hold of my wrist and guided me to stroke his cock. "Shall we take turns, Oliver?" Gabriel's voice seemed to come from far away. "Or will you take his arse while I make use of his mouth?"

"Either," I managed to breathe, "is good with me."

Oliver withdrew his tongue from inside me and I heaved a great breath, trying to get more oxygen into my head. "How about we see if he can get you off with his mouth, and if not you can take his arse after I'm done?" Oliver said. I marvelled at their ability to carry on a relatively civilised conversation. Well, the things they were saying weren't civilised at all, but the tone was.

They were being polite about it, while I fell to pieces between them.

It was so entirely arousing.

Then Oliver's tongue was back inside me, thrusting in and out and making my toes curl. I braced myself with my elbows either side of Gabriel's thighs, readying myself. Gabriel gripped the back of my skull with a firm hand and pulled my face down to his cock. With relish, I opened my mouth and licked at him, tasting the hot sweat and musk of him and loving every bit of him.

I slackened my jaw and took him in my mouth, groaning again as he filled my mouth, pressing quickly on my gag reflex in a way that, again, made my toes curl.

Oliver's tongue retreated and he quickly slicked me with oil before pressing the warm head of his cock against me. I encouraged him, trying to say 'more' around Gabriel's cock.

Gabriel's fingers stroked and combed through my hair, petting me like the dog he sometimes named me for. It was bliss.

I closed my eyes and listened to the two of them, adjusting my knees slightly as Oliver moved closer in, pushing himself deep and making me groan around Gabriel. I pressed my tongue against the musky shaft of him. From the noises they were making they were also enjoying themselves, and possibly kissing.

I swallowed, tipped my chin and took Gabriel as deep into my throat as I could manage, delighting in the raw groan he made as a result. He gripped my head again and started to thrust. I let my jaw go slacker, giving him the power to fuck my face as he wished.

Oliver was moving erratically, thrusting into me with a stuttering rhythm I couldn't predict. I could hear him gasping and panting, his cock filling me, pulling partially out and then shoving in again.

He came without any warning aside from the increasing temperamental nature of his thrusts.

Gabriel pulled out of my throat and positioned his cock just inside my lips as he came, filling my mouth with his deliciousness. I swallowed it down and greedily licked at his cock, cleaning him up and sucking the last traces from him.

"Good work, puppy," he said, his voice gravelly and low.

Oliver slapped my ass as he pulled out, making me yelp with surprise. Then Gabriel's hands were on my shoulders, Oliver's were on my hips, and working in unison they flipped me onto my back. My head in Gabriel's lap, and my legs pressed against Oliver's side.

"Yes, very good," Oliver said, running his hands up my thighs and closing one around my cock which was practically purple with need. I was aroused as Hell, and eager to come, but I was feeling something else as well, a raging fire of appreciation for the two of them.

I was impressed at the way they seemed to be working together, Oliver taking a slight lead from Gabriel, but both of them in easy accord about using me and consensually abusing me. The feeling was hot in my chest, and inexplicably made me want to cry with happiness, but I swallowed it back.

Instead, I let myself feel deliciously overwhelmed as Gabriel leaned down to kiss me on the mouth, his hands dancing over my chest, tweaking my nipples and scratching lightly on my sides. Well, I was overwhelmed with emotions inside already but my body was quickly overcome from the sensations.

I tried to ask permission to come but Gabriel's tongue was so far into my mouth it came out as a vague needy whimper, and I came under Oliver's expert manipulation with no one giving the word.

Oh well, if I'm in trouble for that I'll happily take the punishment I thought, absolutely giddy with the intensity of the orgasm.

Gabriel released my mouth and sat up again, Oliver stroked

my cock, leaning in to lick me clean, teasing around the tip of me and then lapping it off my stomach like some kind of insanely sexy cat.

I moaned my appreciation and hoped I'd be able to use words again soon. I wanted to tell them how much I loved them, but the thought of that put a lump in my throat and I felt my emotions threatening to overwhelm me again.

Oliver sat up and wiped the back of his forearm over his mouth, grinning like a cat who'd got the cream.

"You're amazing," I managed to rasp out. "Both of you."

Gabriel looked down at me, he was upside down from my perspective. He smiled, his blond hair falling into his face. "So are you."

We all shifted around then, so Gabriel was leaning back against the pillows with me under one arm and Oliver under the other, both of us gazing at each other over his chest. It was almost a perfect moment, except that in the back of my head I was still worried about Dante. But I could allow myself some lingering in the moment, catching my breath, tangled in the naked limbs of my two more dominant lovers.

CHAPTER 8

IN WHICH DANTE AND CEDRIC HAVE A
SERIOUS CONVERSATION

*A*n hour or so later I went to find Dante. He was out on the deck, ostensibly being Captain while Gabriel was otherwise occupied, but to my eye he appeared to be brooding. He was on deck near the helm, looking out at the ocean with Gabriel's spyglass. His back was to the ship, and to the merchantman that sailed close beside us, crewed by a few of the captured crew and a few of our men.

In the late Carribean afternoon, his hair shone like the wing of a raven, not just black but purples and blues playing in the hue, intriguing and inviting. But now wasn't the time to wax lyrical about how pretty his hair was, he was upset, and I needed to make amends.

I cleared my throat as I approached, which was probably unnecessary since I'm sure his vampiric powers extended to wolf-like hearing.

His shoulders stiffened but he didn't turn or anything to say hello. "Dante, can we have a word?" I asked, moving to the railing beside him. Although every fibre of my being wanted to touch him or lean on him, I resisted, giving him his space.

He sighed, and lowered the spyglass. "I suppose we had better."

"Wonderful," I said. "So, uh, the whole tattoo thing…" I started.

Dante actually looked at me then. "Perhaps this discussion would be better had in private?"

"Oh, yes, private, good." I smiled a little, not too much because I was still trying to be contrite and get through to him, but in private I knew what to do. I knew what he wanted, which was me, and my body, and I knew how to give that to him. Perhaps this wouldn't be too difficult to solve after all.

He led the way to his cabin below deck and I followed, feeling more and more buoyant by the second.

Once we were in his cabin, I shut the door and went to him. He hadn't sat down, but was standing and watching me, one hand on his jaw and the other crossed over his chest. He looked like the ideal Gothic poet hero of some lurid romance, and my heart thrummed with my desire for him.

"What would you like?" I asked. "Shall I go to my knees and please you, or would you prefer to feed first?"

Dante's eyes narrowed and he shook his head. "I beg your pardon?"

"I want to make it up to you," I said, feeling slightly confused. "How would you like me to do that?"

"I was under the impression we were going to talk," Dante said slowly. I swallowed, suddenly unsure of myself all over again.

"Oh, I thought because you asked me down here you wanted…" I trailed off, because of course he could see what I thought he'd wanted. And I'd already said it all out loud about how to start off. "Right, sorry."

"Cedric…" Dante sighed again. "You thought I was just wanting to have sex with you? And that would stop me being concerned for you?"

"I thought… I thought it would stop you being angry with

me," I said, feebly. I hadn't quite thought of it in those terms before. "I thought I could make it up to you."

"Cedric, I'm not angry with you." Dante dropped his hands to his sides and peered into my face. "I'm terrified. Don't you see that?"

My stomach turned over unpleasantly and something hollow seemed to open in my chest. I didn't like the sensation at all, and I felt like I was rapidly losing control of my understanding. But this was Dante, and I could be open with him. He loved me, after all.

"I know, and I know you said that I shouldn't use the powers, but I can't... I could barely help myself. The man was coming for me and it was instinctive, in a way."

"Instinctive? So you didn't choose to use it? It just happened without your meaning to?" When Dante asked that it sounded so much worse, so I cleared my throat.

"No, I mean, I wanted to, but there wasn't time to stop myself, he was coming right at me and Bilal was on the helm." I pushed my hand through my curls. I wasn't even sure what I was trying to say except that I hadn't been deliberately putting myself in danger. "But I'm sorry. I didn't want to scare you."

Dante took my hand and squeezed it in his cool one. "You're going to keep scaring me, Cedric, I know that, because I care for you, and I love you, and you're... you, so you're going to keep acting without thought."

I swallowed, feeling rather attacked by that, and affronted at his reading of my character. "I don't act without thought. That's a terrible thing to say."

Dante fixed me with a piercing stare and I shook my hand free of his. His expression softened. "Perhaps I misspoke, not as much without thought as on instinct. You react fast and it's not always the best course of action."

How had we ended up talking about this? I thought I was

apologising and then we'd have make up sex, not dissect my
personality.

"I don't know what you want me to say," I said. I felt petulant and childish, being scolded for something I was hardly aware of doing.

Dante frowned, turned away and picked up a bottle of wine. "How about a drink, and we sit down and try and reason out what's happening between us?"

My stomach dropped away and my skin went cold. "Are you... are you going to suggest we separate?" I asked, my voice slightly hoarse.

"I don't believe so," Dante said. He gestured to the bed, and I went and sat on it. He pulled up a chair and poured us each a glass of wine. "But you seem to be assuming some things about us, or perhaps about me, and I'd like to clear the air."

I took the glass he offered me warily, half convinced he was going to tell me he'd never sleep with me again. And that thought rocked me to the core, filled me with a dread I couldn't understand the depth of. I eyed the wine, and then sipped it. The sweet taste flooded my mouth and I was grateful for it, it meant I didn't need to speak.

But of course, Dante had the patience of the devil himself and the silence stretched out unbearably for almost a minute. I became increasingly desperate to fix things.

"I'm truly sorry," I said, pouring my fear of losing him into the words so he'd hear how sincere I was. "I didn't want to scare you, I never did. And I apologise."

"All right," Dante said, his mouth pulling up briefly on one side. "Thank you for your apology."

"And I really thought when you invited me down here it was to have sex," I said, encouraged by the hint of smile I'd seen. "And obviously, it's fine that you don't want to have sex, I just got the wrong message."

"Why did you want to have sex with me when you knew I

was upset with you?" Dante asked, saying each word slowly and carefully. I tilted my head, confused again.

"Because you're Dante and you're hot as fuck?"

"All right, why did you think I wanted to have sex with you, while I was upset with you?" he said, in much the same tone.

"Why? Because that's what we do?" I hadn't intended to phrase this as a question but that's how it came out all the same. I was baffled.

"I wanted to talk." Dante sipped his wine and set it down, resting his elbows on his knees he leaned forward and steepled his fingers. "Cedric, do you think I only like, or indeed, love you because of sex?"

My mouth went dry, because of course I thought that. It was all I had to offer after all, my good looks and my prowess in the bedroom, or outside of it as the case may be. But I knew it wasn't the answer he wanted to hear from me.

"I don't... what else do I have to offer?" I asked, my voice quavering and weak. It sounded hateful to my ears, pathetic, and not at all the kind of man I wanted to be. But Dante had seen through to the core of me, somehow.

I drained my wine, miserable in my skin, set the glass aside and plucked at the bedclothes.

"Cedric." Dante's voice was softer now. "Sunshine. Why do you think I chose that name for you?"

A flash of darkness crossed my mind and I answered before considering. "Because I'm going to hurt you. You just said you're afraid for me, and I'm stupid and reckless, which means I'm going to hurt you someday, just like if you lost your magic charm and went out in daylight."

Dante sighed and I felt his hand on mine, drawing it away from where I was plucking uselessly at the blanket. "Cedric, will you please look at me for a moment?"

I'd been avoiding his gaze but it felt cowardly to do so now. I swallowed and looked up into his deep green eyes. "What?"

"I call you sunshine because you're optimistic, and cheerful and you don't... often... let things get to you. Not like I do. You have a bright way of looking at the world, and I value that very highly."

I squeezed his hand impulsively, not trusting my voice if I were to speak again. Instead I urged him to continue with my eyes.

"I've not told you a great deal about my life before the Devil's Whore," Dante said. "Maybe now would be a good time."

"Maybe it would," I said.

CHAPTER 9

IN WHICH DANTE TALKS OF HIS PAST

*D*ante shuffled his chair a little closer to the bed and sat back in it, dropping my hand and gazing past me for a moment as he thought. Remembered things. I wondered what tidbit he'd share. It was a welcome distraction from talking about how I only had sex to offer, and I hoped the lump in my throat would go away soon. Distraction was what I needed.

"Let's see... Paris, I was at the coffee house, during *foire Saint-Germain* in 1672, I remember because it was the first time a Parisian café was popular enough to stay open, and I enjoyed being there. Now, of course, they're everywhere..."

"Of course," I said. I'd, of course, never been to Paris on account of the recent war, and the ongoing animosity England had for both France and Spain.

"I had been going to all the theatre I could manage, meeting all sorts of fascinating people," he said. "One in particular caught my eye. He was an actor, played the most wonderful Hamlet I've ever seen."

I smirked. "Of course you fell in love with Hamlet. He's just your type, wears black all the time, talks about how sad he is..."

Dante rolled his eyes but his mouth quirked up at the same time. "Well, he wasn't like that off the stage. He was full of light and enthusiasm. What the French call *joie de vivre*, just being in the same room with him was invigorating."

"What was his name?" I liked the way Dante was smiling now, his expression misted with time. He was in some way, back there, looking at this man, as he told me the story.

"Gaspard, the name means treasure, which seemed... well, entirely appropriate for who he was. He had no shortage of admirers, of course, but I was lucky enough to catch his eye."

"Of course you were," I said. "And luck had nothing to do with it, you're handsome and mysterious. I'd wager he was utterly entranced."

Dante smiled, his eyes focusing on mine for a moment. "Perhaps we entranced each other," he said. He breathed out slowly and his eyes went vague again as he remembered. I wished I could paint him just like this, capture the wistful happiness of his expression. If only I could paint something so fleeting...

"Well, what did you two...what happened?" I prompted.

"The two of us had a few wild nights together, perhaps a month's worth, on and off. I took him to dinner, he took me behind the stage to see how they made the ghost appear and disappear. We... well, we made love. I'd been a vampire for a long time before then, but I didn't dare feed from him, he was too precious and too, I don't know, innocent, in a way."

"Innocent?" I smiled and put my hand on Dante's knee.

"Yes, he had a purity of spirit, it's hard to define, I suppose. Once I took him to my apartment and he showed me a dance he learned for a show where he played a woman, a very sensual woman."

My mouth watered, and I realised I wanted more details of exactly what they'd done, but perhaps that wasn't the reason that Dante was telling me about Gaspard. "Go on," I said. "What happened between the two of you?"

"There are a number of vampires in Paris," Dante said. His

expression turned darker. "And like me they were often drawn to the theatre, to the artists and the young who were so full of life."

My stomach dropped and I squeezed his hand. "Gaspard, he went missing one night. I didn't think much of it at first, for we didn't spend every moment together. But when he didn't show up for a performance, that's when I knew something was dreadfully wrong."

"Oh no," I murmured. Sympathetic, but as eager to know what happened next as if Dante were performing a stage show himself.

"He'd been caught, lured by a particularly cruel example of my kind. A minor baron, who thought Paris was his to do with as he liked. From what I could tell, he'd lured Gaspard home with him, possibly entranced him, and drained him dry." Dante paused, swallowed and looked up at me. I had both his hands in mine and I'd moved closer to him, our knees touching. "Gaspard... I don't know what he thought in those last moments, but he didn't deserve that. He had so much more to give. If I'd paid more attention I could have saved him, perhaps. Hell, if I'd told him what I was, then he'd have been more prepared, he could have worn a cross, or spoken Holy words, it might have... no, it *would* have saved his life."

"You can't blame yourself for someone else's actions, though," I said.

"No, I can't, but I can be haunted by how I held back when I didn't have to," Dante said. "I have no intention of making that same mistake again, with you. I am afraid for you, Cedric. There are dangers we don't yet comprehend, and your cursed tattoo is one of them."

My stomach knotted and fell away and I sighed. The story of Gaspard had been affecting, to say the very least, and with the comparison, I could begin to see where Dante was coming from.

"I'm sorry, I do understand that," I said. "And I'm sorry about Gaspard, you must have been heartbroken."

"Yes, I suppose I was," he said. "I found the scoundrel who'd done it and pulled him apart." He said it so casually I thought he might have been joking for a moment, but then it was clear he wasn't. I tried to hide my shudder.

"Well, I dare say it served him right."

"You remind me of Gaspard, obviously," Dante said. "You have the same light in you, your paintings, like his performances, you interest people, you inspire them. Do you really think that your body is just that to Oliver? Or to Gabriel?"

I bit my lip and swallowed the lump that had appeared in my throat once more. "I know Oliver knows me, and loves me anyway," I said.

"What do you mean by saying anyway?" Dante's voice had dropped lower.

"I mean, despite all my shortcomings. He knows I'm hopeless, that I don't think clearly, that I'm a rake and free with myself. He knows all that, and he loves me anyway, that's precious to me."

Dante pulled me into his lap abruptly and wrapped his arms around me, pulling me close, and encircling me securely. "Cedric, why do you think your flaws, or indeed, your choice of behaviour, makes you unworthy of love?"

I opened my mouth but I had no words, no way to respond to that. I made a non-committal wordless sound.

He smiled and kissed the corner of my mouth. "Look at it this way, would you think I'm unlovable because I pulled another vampire apart?"

"Of course not, you're a pirate, and a vampire, of course you're going to kill people and drink their blood. I love you." It was getting easier to say those three words to him, although I still had butterflies about it.

"So, my actions aren't what you love or hate about me?"

I swallowed, because it seemed like a sort of false

equivalency. "It's not the same, though. You have so much more to offer."

Dante pressed his forehead to mine and looked into my eyes. I went cross eyed very fast and my eyes watered. "Cedric, you are a ray of light, you're creative, you're funny and captivating. Trust me, if you decided to stop having sex with me right now, I'd still want to hang around you and talk to you and get to know you better."

I inhaled, feeling raw and a bit sad all of a sudden. Dante let the silence stretch out before he spoke again.

"Do you believe me? Do you think I'm telling you the truth?"

I searched inside me for the answer. But my gut knew Dante wouldn't lie. "Yes, I believe that."

"Well, that's something." He kissed me gently. "Think about it, Cedric."

I nodded and rubbed my cheek against his, feeling raw and open.

CHAPTER 10

IN WHICH CEDRIC VISITS TORTUGA AND A WITCH, AGAIN

The Devil's Whore docked in Tortuga on what appeared to be a quiet day. The moorings were largely empty, only a half dozen ships instead of the thirty or more that had been there the last time we visited.

"Some days are like this," Gabriel said, handing me his hat to hold as he combed his hair back into a stubby ponytail at the back of his head. I turned his hat over in my hands, admiring the workmanship.

"You don't think it's a bad sign, then?" Oliver asked. He'd been seated at the desk in Gabriel's cabin, working on notes or observations or something.

"There may've been an attempted raid or similar," Gabriel said. "But more likely it's just that everyone's elsewhere doing other things. I've sent Marco out first to scout before we disembark, just in case."

Dante appeared in the doorway, apparently he'd just pressed his satin breeches, or something, because he looked absolutely perfect. "I don't sense anything particularly untoward, if that helps," he said.

Gabriel glanced at him, took his hat back off me and settled it on his head, checking the angle of it in his looking glass.

"Well, that's good to know," Gabriel said. "I don't think it's a bad sign, but it never hurts to be cautious."

A few minutes later, after I'd made Dante give me several kisses, there was a cry on the deck from Kaito.

"All clear, Marco's signalled."

"Wonderful," Gabriel said. "Shall we, then?"

He offered me his arm, which I took. "That's a very gallant gesture, Gabriel," I said, pleased.

He chuckled. "Well, one of these days I might need to take you to a dance or ball or similar, might as well practise now. Are you coming, Oliver?"

I wasn't sure when Gabriel had switched from calling Oliver 'mister Stanhope" to his first name, but I liked it as a progression.

"Yes," Oliver said. He stood up from the desk and he and Dante followed us out. Of course, Gabriel could hardly keep hold of my arm as we went down the gangplank, but it felt appropriately grand as we walked across the deck.

"I'll take care of selling the Green Knight, with Marco's assistance," Gabriel said. "Then I'll head to the Pickled Oyster for rooms, meet you there?"

"I'd like to check in on Tanith," I said. "If that's all right? I mean, the way the tattoo's changed, and all. I'd like to see what they think of it."

"Fine with me." Gabriel nodded. "Dante, keep an eye on him, will you?"

"Naturally," Dante said. "I'd like to see them, too."

"And I'll tag along," Oliver added. He had his notebook and pen under his arm, his glasses had fallen down his nose, and he looked every inch the plucky scholar out to investigate the natural world. Or something like that, anyway. My heart thumped with affection for him and I slipped my hand into his.

"Fine, then you'll see I'm well taken care of." I went up on my toes to peck Gabriel on the lips and then we turned to go.

The streets of Tortuga looked much the same as our last visit, if not a bit quieter. There were still ruffians of every kind, and people sitting in their doorways and going about their business. It was a strange kind of relaxation to be had here. You could do just about anything freely, no one looked twice at partners of the same sex, or multiple partners come to that, but you had to keep a weather eye on your purse and your back, in case someone was feeling opportunistic.

As we made our merry way to the street where Tanith had their shop, I felt rather pleased with myself. There I was, well dressed, with two of my lovers flanking me, on a sunny day that promised drinks and fine food at the inn, followed by all sorts of antics, perhaps with all three of my lovers if I was lucky?

But when we came to Tanith's front door my elation vanished. The door was broken, half off its hinges and the window was clouded with soot.

"Uh, hello?" I called out. I stepped forward and tapped on the broken door. "Anyone in?"

There was no response. I peered in through the doorframe to see the store was ruined. Burned out, the walls blackened and the merchandise strewn across the floor.

"That's not good," Oliver murmured.

I felt a thrill of fear over what might have happened to them.

"Cedric, let me," Dante said. He pulled me gently back by the elbow and stepped inside. He sniffed the air and vanished inside. "Wait there, it might not be safe," he said, from somewhere in the darkness.

I turned to look at Oliver in exasperation. "It never stops does it? The 'stay where it's safe', thing?"

Oliver shrugged. "Well, if the place was burned it might be structurally unsound now. Dante's pretty unlikely to suffer from something falling on him, isn't that right?"

I frowned. "Well, I suppose."

"And he doesn't need to breathe the same way we do, so inhaling soot and ash won't bother him but it might choke us."

I sighed and pushed a hand through my curls. "Will you kindly stop being so calm and reasonable and let me complain?"

Oliver smiled with no apparent regret and winked at me.

Urgh, he's so entirely adorable, I can't even be properly annoyed at him.

I huffed and looked away, trying to stop my mouth from smiling even though it kept pulling up. I went to look in the window to distract myself. While the glass was smeared with soot, the lettering on the window was still largely intact, the paint only peeling here and there. I couldn't see much though.

I hated seeing Tanith's place like this, though. It made me feel sick in my stomach, worry, I supposed. I hoped they hadn't been hurt at all.

Dante came out the front door again, looking troubled. He had something in his hand and held out to me. "Recognise this?"

It looked like a small, slim feather, with an olive cast to it. About four inches long and slender, far too small to use for a quill.

I shook my head. "Not at all."

"I don't remember any of the witches at the ritual they did for you using any kind of bird or animal companion."

I took it from him and turned it over in my hands, shaking my head. "No, neither. There were a lot of herbs, potions... crystals of course. But nothing like this."

"A lot of the wares are gone from the store," Dante said. "I'm not sure if that means it's been looted or if Tanith got out with some of their things."

Oliver took the feather off me and examined it. "Does this have a particular significance?"

"Well, it's not smudged with soot or anything for one. It

might be a clue as to who did this," Dante said. "It looks to me like something a sorcerer might use." As he said it, his lip curled into a sneer. He clearly didn't think much of sorcerers. I tried to remember what I knew of them.

"*Orthotomus sutorius* if I'm not mistaken," Oliver said. "Not a native to anywhere near here, they're usually found in the more tropical parts of Asia."

"A what, now?" I asked, peering over his shoulder at it as if I'd suddenly be able to understand.

"Tailorbird," Oliver said, looking at me briefly and turning the feather this way and that. "Named that way because they construct their nests by sewing together large leaves to make a sort of tent. They tie knots, almost, using the plant fibers. Fascinating species, I've only read about them and seen paintings, but I'm relatively sure that's what it's from."

When Oliver got going on something he'd studied it made my knees weak, so I cleared my throat to get the conversation back onto something distinctly unsexy. "So, a sorcerer you think, Dante?" My voice cracked a little.

"Sorcerers… they're not naturally magical, isn't that right? They get their power from an external being," Oliver said. He handed the delicate feather back to Dante, who slipped it into his breast pocket.

"That's right."

"So, they're different from witches, who have magic naturally. Which means, what, they're enemies?" I suggested.

"Not necessarily," Dante said. "As with many things it depends on who is involved. People sometimes hate each other, of course, but it's not like a natural enemy situation. Which begs the question of why someone would attack Tanith."

Oliver and Dante both looked at me significantly. I stuck my hands into the pockets of my trousers. "What? You think it was the cult?"

"It could have been," Dante said. "We know it is largely nobles with a lot of money, they could have hired a sorcerer."

I frowned, and looked at the broken door of the house. I hated to think I could be in some way responsible for bad fortune coming to Tanith and the other witches who lived in the area. I felt my shoulders tighten and hunch.

"But we don't really know anything," Oliver said, a little too late to make me feel better.

"I'm sure there's some way we can find out," Dante said. "I'll put the word out that we're looking for them and see what happens."

"Let's see if Gabriel's at the inn, shall we?" Oliver looped his arm through mine.

CHAPTER 11

IN WHICH NATALIA HARROW RESEARCHES
AND BROODS

*N*atalia Harrow was studying the book of the Unknowable, checking her late brother's translations were correct in the study of the governor's house. It was late afternoon and she'd been at work on it most of the day. To her irritation, there were few errors in Rupert's work, but the few she did find were rather important definitions, and so she had to keep checking in case there were worse ones.

Naberus had been sauntering in and out of the study all day, and it was beginning to irritate her. He walked in again and stood nearby, sighing. She set down her pen and cleared her throat.

"Is there something bothering you, Naberus?"

"The boy is out there still," he said. He didn't look at her, but gazed out the window at the view of the harbour. The sails on the distant horizon.

"I know the boy is out there," she said, shortly.

"And something else as well," he said. This was the first Natalia had heard of something else. She rose from the chair and walked towards the tall, strange man-shaped thing.

"Something else? What are you talking about?"

"Something, or perhaps, someone, has started to move, their plans seem to be counter to our own, they are perhaps also pursuing the boy."

Natalia folded her arms and drummed a finger impatiently on her upper arm. "What do you know, spit it out, Nab. I don't like your vagueness. You said we had time."

"We had time previously. That was before this... thing... happened," he said.

"What thing?"

He turned to look at her, his eyes flashing with an unearthly green light. "I don't have details. I only know that there's a shift in the magical fabric of things. Perhaps if you would allow me to wander, I could go to the source of the shift and see for myself."

Natalia, oblivious to the face that Naberus had already been travelling on his own, and that he wasn't nearly as bound to her as she thought, pursed her lips. "Why should I allow you such freedom? Perhaps you would use it to work against me yourself, or warn my enemies as to my location."

Naberus's face melted into a warm, reassuring smile. "My dear Mistress," he said. "I have only ever served you and your goals. It hurts me to hear you don't trust me." Nab took Natalia's hand and fixed her with his gaze. "You should let me do as I will."

Natalia's breath caught and she swallowed. For a moment it appeared as if she might fight his suggestion, but Nab pushed a little harder with his magic and her expression relaxed.

"Of course I trust you, Nab. I allow you to travel, to see what this thing is. Find out what you can, and what our best course of action will be. I'll see if I can't find a ship in case we have to leave."

"If you think it best, Mistress," Nab said, lowering his eyes and playing bashful. "I shall go and be back within two hours."

Natalia squeezed his hand and kissed his cheek. "But make sure to return to me," she said. "That's an order, Naberus."

"Yes, Mistress."

She released his hand and he walked out of the room, waiting until he was out of her line of sight before vanishing to travel faster than the speed of light via the astral plane.

CHAPTER 12

IN WHICH ENQUIRIES ARE MADE AND AN OLD FRIEND FOUND

The Pickled Oyster, much like the rest of the island, wasn't as busy as it had been when we'd visited a few weeks earlier. Gabriel had set himself up at the large corner table, and Dante, Oliver and I joined him for drinks and food.

"How was the witch?" Gabriel asked. Before I could answer he tugged me in for a kiss and for a moment I forgot everything except how much I liked the Captain. But as soon as the kiss was done the unsettled feeling returned to my stomach.

"Gone," I said. "It looked as if their store had been burned out."

"That's, well, that's a shame, but it's hardly unheard of in Tortuga."

"The other shops on the road looked unharmed," Oliver added. He reached over the table and snagged one of the chicken wings on the plate in front of Gabriel. Gabriel watched him do it and didn't react.

"It did appear to be a targeted attack," Dante said. "And there was a token left from... well, perhaps from the culprit although we can't be sure."

"Mm." Gabriel beckoned the waiter over, a handsome young

man with tightly curled deep brown hair. "More chicken, please, and another jug of wine."

"Is there any of that divine bread?" I asked and the man nodded, giving me a quick smile.

"Yes, of course."

"Yes, two orders of that, some of that garlic shrimp dish, and how about a plate of steamed vegetables as well. This lot are on the brink of scurvy, most likely," Gabriel joked. The waiter nodded and went back behind the counter.

"We are not on the brink of scurvy," Oliver said. He sucked a chicken bone clean and reached for another.

"You're on the brink of something, Mister Stanhope." Gabriel's lips were smiling but there was that exciting flash in his eye that promised delicious things like ropes and pain. My trousers were suddenly too tight.

Just imagine if I got to see Gabriel dominating Oliver, oh stars, that would almost be enough to make me orgasm without being touched.

"All right, sunshine?" Dante asked, softly. He was sitting on my other side. "Your heart sped up."

"Mmhm! Just fine," I said. The waiter returned with chilled glasses and I snatched one up to press it to my suddenly hot cheek.

"I'll go out in a moment," Dante said. "To ask around about what happened to Tanith's store. Someone must know something, and I expect my contacts will know more than most."

I turned to look at him directly, forgetting my sudden arousal. "Would you like me to come with you? I feel somewhat responsible, after all."

"No, not this time. My friends here are sometimes strange about... humans. Like you. If I can find anything I'll be back immediately to let you know."

I leaned against his arm and frowned. "Right, of course."

Gabriel dug in his pocket and produced two room keys, tossed one to Dante and put the other on the table in front of Oliver. "Since they're so quiet I got a deal on rooms. One each for each of us, except Cedric of course, he can pick where he sleeps."

I smiled, because although some part of me wanted to be treated the same as the others, and afforded my own room, I also knew I wouldn't use it. I was far too used to sleeping with company now, and I didn't want to give up a rare opportunity to sleep on land with one or more of my lovers.

"Mm, my choice..." I said, stretching my arms up over my head so that my shirt rode up a little and a sliver of stomach was revealed to those watching. "However can I make such an important decision?"

Oliver pulled the fresh, steaming plate of garlic shrimp towards him, they appeared to be absolutely swimming in melted butter. "Well, you won't want this on your breath, will you? Best you eat your vegetables to aid your brain."

I stuck my tongue out at him. "Well, if you're eating all that I won't be choosing you."

Dante chuckled and started slicing the bread, passing out heavy slices of it. It smelled absolutely heavenly, fresh and good. I slathered mine with butter.

Gabriel helped himself to the vegetables and then passed the plate to me. In no time I had a plate heaped with a little of everything, even some garlic shrimp Oliver reluctantly shared. Dante ate a single piece of bread and then excused himself to make his enquiries.

A couple of hours later, Dante returned. I, by this time, was pleasantly tipsy on wine and food, and sitting in Gabriel's lap. Marco and Kaito had joined us, and made short work of our leftovers.

Kaito had been regaling us with a story about a sea serpent that I wasn't entirely sure was true. But when I saw that Dante had someone with him I jumped off Gabriel's lap and Kaito trailed off.

"I'll want to hear the rest of this later," I said. "But I think I'm needed."

Dante's companion was someone I recognised immediately. A beautiful, tall and impressive witch who had been present at the ritual Tanith had held for me.

"Adianez," I said. I smiled and held my hand out to shake, she looked at it with one arched eyebrow and then took my fingers in hers briefly. I wondered if there wasn't some unspoken rule about greeting witches that I should have known about.

"Cedric, it's good to see you alive," she replied.

"Why don't the three of us sit down?" Dante suggested. He led the way to a table towards the wall. He pulled a chair out for Adianez, she ignored it, and sat in a seat on the other side of the table. Dante caught my eye and shrugged, nodding to me. I took the seat and Dante gallantly pushed the chair in. He sat beside me. Oliver appeared from across the room.

"So, you're looking for Tanith, I take it?" Adianez said. She leaned closer in, lowering her voice. "They're all right, they just fled the sorcerer. They're on one of the outlying islands, biding their time at the moment."

"The sorcerer," I looked at Dante. "That's what you thought it could be."

Adianez nodded slowly. "I was staying with Tanith, after the ritual. We spent some time together, so I was there when it happened. I'd seen an omen in the sunrise, so we knew there would be trouble of some kind."

"I beg your pardon, if I could just interrupt for a moment. I might just... Would you like a drink?" Dante asked, as the waiter came by. Adianez shook her head, and Dante waved the waiter off.

"As I was saying, we were slightly on edge and we didn't know exactly what form the trouble would take. Sometimes it's simply a rude customer, or a dropped teacup. But on that morning it was far worse."

Adianez paused, licked her lips and gazed at Dante. "Perhaps I would like a lemon tea?"

"Of course," Dante got to his feet. "Cedric?"

"Uh, yes, sounds good," I said. I swallowed, annoyed with all these interruptions. "So the sorcerer came by?"

"He was looking for you, Cedric." Adianez leaned in, her eyes flashing. "He wanted the boy with the tattoo, and he knew your full name."

A chill went down my spine. "Did... did you get his name?" I asked, possibly quite stupidly.

Adianez shook her hair out. "No. He demanded information of Tanith and when they refused to answer, he set the place alight. His familiar was a small bird, a little green thing, quite odd looking with a longish beak."

I sighed and sat back in the chair and shrugged. "As far as I'm aware, I've never met a sorcerer at all, let alone one with a small green bird."

"He certainly seemed to know you."

Dante returned with the tea and poured it for both myself and Adianez. "If you could give us quite a detailed description perhaps that would help?"

"He was an older man, pale and white, almost sickly looking, if it weren't for the magic. I could see it coursing through him, giving him power." Adianez tapped her finger against her teacup. "His accent was English but with a distinctly Caribbean touch to it, perhaps he's from one of the larger British ports."

"Well, if he knew me, it's possible he was from Kingston," I said. "I wasn't there all that long but I did make rather an impression, if you know what I mean?" I flashed my teeth in a charming smile but Adianez just blinked at me in response.

"He appeared quite unremarkable," she said. "Aside from the bird familiar and his link to strange magics of course."

"Go on," Dante said, slowly. "Cedric could attempt to sketch his likeness? He's quite talented at faces."

I smiled, flushed with pride at Dante's having noticed my skills with charcoal. "Oh, that might be all right," I said. "I left all my sketching things on the boat of course, but..."

"I have nothing else I need to do tonight," Adianez said.

"How long ago did this happen?" I asked. I sipped my tea but it was too hot still and it scorched my tongue.

"Almost two weeks ago," Adianez said. "Tanith has gone to another island, one with more mountains. They like to dig around in the caves for more crystals... it grounds them I suppose. They're quite all right, and in time they will come back and restore the shop. In the meantime I've been keeping an eye over it remotely."

"Two weeks, there's no chance he'd still be on the island, is there?" I turned to Dante, who looked rather concerned.

"Let me tell Gabriel," he said, quickly. "He will decide on our course of action." Dante rose from the table and crossed the room to Gabriel.

"Are you going to get your drawing things?" Adianez asked. I shrugged.

"Rather depends on what the Captain says, I suppose. But honestly, there were a lot of boring old white men in Kingston, I imagine one would look much the same as the others."

She nodded sagely. "Indeed." I picked up my tea again and blew on it, my mind working.

"And he's almost certainly involved with the same ridiculous cult we already know about. They're all right at using magic, although there hasn't been a sorcerer yet, it might just be the new angle Harrow is using to try and get to me."

Adianez looked me over and frowned suddenly. "What happened to your protection?"

"Oh, fuck, it got smashed." I leaned forward, feeling a sudden urgency. "Do you think you could make me another one? I'd be really grateful."

"I can't make one with all the different magics combined," she said. "But I can certainly mix up some ointments for you, if you're not sailing off on the next tide that is. And I'm sure there's salvageable crystals in Tanith's shop. I haven't looked too deeply into what's remaining as it will be *such* a tiresome clean up job."

Dante returned to the table. "Gabriel wishes to stay at least two more days, but he wants you to stay close, Cedric. Perhaps not even leave the inn."

I shrugged and smiled. "Fine with me, just means someone else will need to retrieve my drawing things."

"I'll bring them."

"Right." Adianez downed her tea. I sipped at mine but I still found it far too hot. "I'll see you tomorrow then, expect me at midday. I'll get something brewing for you, and bring what I can. Then you can try drawing this man from my description."

"Thank you so much," Dante said. He offered her his arm as she got up from the table and she eyed him before taking it. The two of them talked softly as they left the inn. I picked up my teacup and took it back over to where the others were having a rollicking good time without me.

CHAPTER 13

IN WHICH CAPTAIN LUCIFER STAKES HIS CLAIM

I didn't stay down in the common area much longer at all. In fact, once I rejoined the group, Gabriel pushed the remains of my plate of food towards me and bid me eat.

"Quickly now," he said.

"Everything all right?" Oliver asked, eying me.

I shrugged one shoulder. "Probably? Adianez is coming back tomorrow with some more protection thingies, and she's going to describe the sorcerer so I can draw him."

Gabriel slipped his arm around my waist, which necessitated him shifting his chair towards mine, which felt like an utterly un-Gabriel-like thing to do. Usually it was all him pulling me towards where he was. I didn't hate the change.

"Once you've eaten your fill we're going upstairs," he said, low. "I don't like the thought of you out here in plain sight."

"The dining room is largely empty," I pointed out, not entirely unreasonably I thought.

"Yes, well, call it a gut instinct," he said.

"I might turn in early as well," Oliver said. "There's a bookshop a few doors down that I'd like to get to as soon as it opens, and I have a letter to send back to London. May as well get them both done first thing."

"Dante's gone to the ship, I think." I wiped my mouth with a napkin and gave Gabriel a smile. "To get my drawing things."

"Well, perhaps if he's back in time he can join us," Gabriel said. "Quite finished?"

"No dessert?"

"I'll give you some dessert," he said, his smile promising all sorts of things that sent shivers through me.

"If you insist. Then fine, let's go, since you're in such a great hurry."

All three of us got up from the table and went upstairs. At the top of the stairs I kissed Oliver goodnight and then went into Gabriel's room with him.

He closed the door fast behind me, locked it and then paced into the room. I became aware that he had a tension to him, a sort of dangerous aura speaking to me in a rather carnal way.

I cleared my throat. "Is uh, is everything quite all right?"

He turned to look at me with a flash in his eyes and growled softly. "No. I am utterly sick of everyone trying to take you from me."

I swallowed and slowly walked closer to him. "No one is trying to take me right this second, are they?" I let the double entendre hang in the air, an invitation that I felt quite confident he'd accept.

Remember when he was resisting you, telling you it wasn't right? How far you've both come since then...

He smirked at me.

Licked his lips.

I watched the pinkness of his tongue and felt my mouth water.

"Who do you belong to, Cedric?" His voice was low and gravelly. I, because I love to get myself into trouble, knew the answer but decided not to give it.

"Well, there's Dante, of course, and Oliver. I rather think Oliver would like to say he owns me." As I spoke, my cock swelled and I reached down to adjust my trousers. Gabriel's eyes followed the movement and lingered on my crotch.

Without warning he was upon me, bearing me down to the bed with one hand on my wrist and the other wrapped around my waist. My back hit the bed and I made an involuntary 'oof' sound, and he was on top of me. His mouth on my jaw and nipping at my throat.

"Try again."

I coughed, rocking my hips up against him to make us both moan with need. Of course, he wanted me to be good, to say his name, and submit to him like usual, but something in me sparked against it this evening. This evening I wanted to make him work for it, to prove to me that I should submit. I wanted him to hurt me and show me his strength.

"It's... hard to speak when you're doing that," I wheedled, closing my eyes and swallowing another moan as he sucked a mark into my neck.

He sat up, his eyes blazing blue fire, and tore my shirt open. He yanked it off my arms, grabbed my wrist and pinned me to the bed. "You're trying my patience, puppy. If you want to find release tonight, you'll answer my question."

"You wouldn't..." I said it before I caught myself, and then I bit my tongue, because of course having said that I had given him the upper hand. He knew I wanted it now, and he could use it against me. Well, of course I wanted to orgasm.

"I would, and I'd leave you chained to the bed so you couldn't touch yourself as I slept," he said. His voice was full of dreadful promise, and I almost wanted to test him, to see how it felt to be deprived and chained all night... but my cock won out.

"Fine, I belong to you, Captain," I said, sighing a little.

He let go of my wrists and scratched the nails of both hands down my chest. "Say it like you mean it, if you please."

I swallowed, looked him up and down and once again felt my mouth water. I would never get sick of looking at his muscled chest, at the scars that simply served to accentuate his natural beauty. At the near angelic halo of blond hair and those intense, icy blue eyes. He made me so weak. When I spoke again, the words were full of emotion.

"I belong to you, Gabriel Durant, or Captain Lucifer if that's what you prefer. I'm yours."

He smiled then, a true smile finally, one of relief and indulgence and triumph. He crashed his mouth to mine hard enough my teeth rattled, and I wrapped my arms around him and we kissed as if we would never cease.

He rolled us over, using both hands to tear my trousers open and shove them down my hips. I pulled away from the kiss long enough to pull his shirt open, lifting my hips so he could rid himself of his trousers as well. The two of us were panting, desperate for each other, and it felt like there was no time for our usual preparation or foreplay.

Out of nowhere I remembered our first time together. *How hot and intense and urgent it had all felt on that day. It hardly feels less urgent now, even though we've done this a number of times since.*

I broke the kiss. "Do you remember the first time we fucked?"

"Mm." Gabriel didn't seem inclined to talk. His hands were busy, finding the little pot of coconut oil and slicking his fingers to fuck me with them.

"You told me to be quiet," I said. Then I groaned and shoved my hips down, my toes curling as his fingers filled me. He scissored them, making me whimper with need.

"You didn't listen." He sat up, closed his mouth around my nipple and sucked hard. I whimpered louder, rocking my hips to encourage him to go faster. "The most reliable way to shut you up is this."

He pulled his fingers out, and I groaned, feeling the loss of them, but I didn't have long to wait. He guided his cock to my entrance and pushed inside, slick with more oil.

"Oh fucking Hell," I gasped. I tossed my head back and sank down on him, undulating my hips like one of the dancers I'd seen perform in the most salacious shows.

Gabriel's mouth found my other nipple and his teeth scraped the sensitive skin there. I braced myself with one arm around his shoulders and the other on his thigh as I worked myself up and down.

I tried to remember what I'd been saying, some point I'd been trying to prove to him or to myself. Maybe I was just feeling nostalgic? I felt my heart swell and affection threaten to swamp me with sentimentality.

Not the time, for fucks sake, focus on his cock.

I bounced, slid my hand up his neck to grip his hair and pull him up for another kiss and he growled as he returned it. His arms wrapped tight around me and he rolled on top, pressing me down into the bed and pounding his hips against mine.

I reached a hand up to brace myself on the bedhead, giving myself more strength to push back as he pushed inside me. He took this as the encouragement it was. Closing his hand on my other wrist and pinning it to the pillow, he thrust deep inside and groaned, near to coming. His other hand found my cock and with three deft movements he had me writhing and bucking under him.

"Please, fuck, please please..." I gasped.

"Do it for me," he said. Then he lowered his head to suck another mark into my throat. The sting of his mouth, the fullness of him inside me, the sweat dripping off him and onto me and his firm grip on my arm, they all combined into one glorious sensation and I orgasmed hard.

His mouth opened and I felt his rasping breath, a gasp on my skin as he responded in kind, his seed filling me deliciously.

He thrust a few more times, let go of my wrist and then just sort of collapsed on top of me. I put my arms around him and held on, gasping for air but loving the weight of him on top of me. It felt secure, comforting. I was covered by my tall, handsome pirate captain, and I knew he wanted me to be his. I closed my eyes and smiled, nuzzling my nose into his hair and inhaling the rum, the sweat and the faint smell of lavender.

I bit back the words threatening to pop out. I swallowed them down. Now wasn't the time. I knew Gabriel wanted my body, I knew that. Dante's words echoed in the back of my head, suggesting maybe he liked me for more than sex, but I didn't dare believe it. Gabriel wanted to protect me, he wanted to own me, but those were fleeting I was sure.

Love? I knew Gabriel loved his ship and his crew, and for the moment I was part of those things. For the moment, that would do.

CHAPTER 14

IN WHICH CEDRIC DREAMS

*N*ab stood before me. I couldn't remember how I'd got there, but I was back at the ritual chamber in the governor's house in St Vincent. The wooden cross was behind me but I wasn't chained to it, there was no one in the room except for me and Nab, but there was the lingering smell of incense in the air and I felt immediately concerned.

I raised a palm towards Nab, warning him back. "Don't come any closer..."

"There's nothing to be concerned about," he said. "You weren't with the ship, so I made a safe space for the both of us to meet."

"How is this a safe space?" I cried, my voice cracking some. "This is literally the place you and Natalia Harrow tried to kill me!"

"It's a place we both know," Nab said. "Please, we're not even really here. It's a psychic space I constructed so we could talk."

"You say that as if it explains things," I said. I scrubbed my hand over my forehead and willed myself to wake up. "Am I asleep?"

"Of course," Nab said. "In a manner of speaking."

I groaned, annoyed, and looked around. "Please let me wake up?"

"I can," he said. "But I thought you might like to know that Natalia Harrow is not the only person after you, now."

"I know that!" I cried. I looked back at him and shook my head. "Look, please, just say what you have to say and let me be?"

Nab tutted his tongue against his teeth and shook his head. "Cedric, I'm here to help you. I know you've used your powers again, and I know that nothing bad has happened as a result. I can help you. You have this power, and it's a power that others covet."

"None of this is news."

Nab smiled wider. "The one who follows you, he's not related to the Cult of the Unknowable Way. Well, he was, but he's struck out on his own, made a deal with something unworldly."

"Sounds like Harrow," I said. I looked him up and down. "Remind me where exactly you come from, would you? Oh that's right, you've never said."

"I'm from everywhere and nowhere," Nab said. He spread his arms wide and smiled as if he were welcoming me to a party. I glanced about, nervous suddenly that there might be more people waiting to emerge from the shadows, or from nothingness, summoned by his words.

"That's not an answer," I said. I wondered about how irritating I was finding him. Previously when we spoke on the deck of the ship I'd felt more at ease, more like he was a friend. Now I saw him as alien, as an enemy that couldn't be understood or trusted. Too late I thought I should have hidden my annoyance, and let him think I was going along with whatever he wanted. I bit my tongue. Maybe Gabriel was right and I really did need to learn patience, or restraint, or whatever it is he was always saying.

Nab's tongue flicked out and he narrowed his eyes. "I come from beyond, where the mighty king Azathoth rests. He's my father."

My mouth dropped open. I knew he was something to do with Azathoth of cause, but not that they were actually closely related.

"All right, and you want him brought through into our universe because you want to host a family reunion or something?"

Nab shrugged, and for a moment his smile wavered, but it was for such a brief moment I wasn't sure if I'd imagined it. "Many want the power he would bestow on the one who draws him through."

"Tell me, exactly what will ... he... do when he comes through? Because from what I've heard, and what I've felt, it doesn't really seem like Azathoth is going to come through and just go around bestowing powers and good feelings on people."

I hated saying the name Azathoth out loud. I glanced up, half expecting to see the stars and the horrible thing behind the stars coming closer. But we were still in the large ballroom of the house in St Vincent. My skin felt creepy though, so I crossed my arms over my chest.

It looked as though Nab was a little disturbed as well, his smile had faded. "Well, no, when he comes through he will destroy humankind and everything they've built. He will usher in a new age, one of chaos and unpredictability."

I crossed my arms a little tighter. It was hard to see why any human would want that. "And that's what you want, too?"

Nab blinked. "Of course not, my goals are different to those."

"Listen, why are you here, talking to me?"

"I know this might be hard to understand, but I care about you, Cedric."

I frowned. "That is exceptionally hard to believe."

"It's true. You and I are connected, through the ritual and from Natalia's work."

I shuddered and looked away, because although I knew that Nab was bad news, I couldn't deny that he had been giving me information, seemingly helping me. And some part of me did feel something for him too. Not attraction, exactly, but an affinity perhaps. I didn't want to explore that particularly, even if I did like the help he was giving me.

"Just... is that everything you wanted to say? Because I'd like to wake up again, now. Please."

"Don't let them forget how powerful you are," Nab said. "They're taking you for granted. That's all I want you to keep in mind."

He waved his hand as I opened my mouth to refute him, but then I was in bed in the inn room. It felt like the very small hours, the place was silent, and Gabriel had rolled onto his back. I turned over to face him, resting my cheek on his shoulder and went back to sleep.

CHAPTER 15

IN WHICH WE SAY FAREWELL TO TORTUGA ONCE MORE

Since I'd had such an enjoyable evening the night before, and then that strange dream, I had a sleep in. When I woke up I told Gabriel about the strangeness of the dream. He was already awake, reading a book with an arm slung carelessly around me.

"You think it was a... another one of those visions?" Gabriel asked.

I sat up and leaned my shoulder against his. "I'm not sure, but it did feel kind of real the way the old ones did.

"You dreamed about him... and what did he say to you?"

"He said there wasn't just Harrow and the cult now. That someone else is after me now and we have to be extra vigilant."

Gabriel sat up, sighed and ran a hand through his hair. "That's... well, with that man looking for you a few weeks ago and now this intelligence, it's too dangerous to stay. We'll sail on the evening tide. But I am going to have a long bath this morning and wash my hair."

"Want some help?" I kissed his cheek.

"Sure, I always need someone to scrub my back for me."

Later, we went down to the dining hall for a late breakfast or, possibly early lunch. Dante was already down there and he had a canvas bag that looked to contain my drawing supplies. I sat down beside him and kissed him good morning. "Have you seen Oliver this morning?"

Dante shook his head. "I haven't, but he had early errands didn't he?"

"He did." I felt a little worry in my stomach, but I dismissed it. I had no reason to suspect that anything untowards had happened to Oliver. He could look after himself, I knew that, and he was going to a bookshop and the postal office, what harm could possibly befall him?

The waiter brought over toasted slices of their thick bread, jam, and butter and I got stuck into eating, feeling suddenly ravenous.

Once Adianez arrived, I cleared the plates aside and pulled out my sketch pad, getting to work on a basic face shape before she started to describe the man.

Gabriel watched for a moment, then got up. "I'm going to leave you to it, I think." He kissed my forehead and wandered to the verandah where a couple of crew members from the Devil's Whore were talking to some people I didn't recognise. Friends, from the tones of the voices, and the frequent laughter.

"No, his brow was more lowered, like this..." I looked up and Adianez frowned, pulling her eyebrows down and together.

I adjusted the drawing to match it. When we got to the nose, I started to think I might recognise the man but I couldn't exactly place from where. Was he some friend of my Father's perhaps?

Oliver walked into the inn, looking excited but rumpled, as if he'd perhaps spent an hour or two trying to follow rabbits down their burrows.

"Good afternoon," he said, cheery. He sat down across from me and craned his neck to look at the picture. "Isn't that your old tailor?"

I dropped the stick of charcoal and slapped my hand over

my forehead, no doubt giving myself a nice big black smudge there. "Of course it is. What was his name again? Phillips. Mr Victor Phillips."

"So you do know him?" Adianez said.

"Yes, he made my clothes when I lived in Kingston. He was damn good at it, too."

She curled her lip. "A tailor? Why should a tailor turn sorcerer? It's not like it's hard to find work as a tailor."

I bit my lip, wondering if he'd somehow been using the last piece he'd made for me to keep tabs or track me somehow. My peacock blue brocade coat... I didn't get much opportunity to wear it but I did love it so.

Oliver cocked his head to one side. "Do people become sorcerers for the money?"

"For personal gain," Adianez. "Usually, at least. Money, or fortune of another kind, a title, or to gain power."

"Maybe he just didn't want to make shirts anymore," I said, softly. I thought back to the last time I'd seen the man and how strange it had been. He'd been agitated, especially at the thought of me leaving the island. As if it was news he hadn't been expecting and certainly didn't want to hear.

I'd thought it was odd, but... was he planning something all that time ago?

He hadn't been at the Hellfire club, I was fairly sure of that. But then, why follow me here?

"He wasn't a sorcerer back then was he? How would I even be able to tell?"

"He'd have had his bird with him," Adianez said. "A Sorcerer cannot move more than a few metres from their familiar."

Oliver looked around Adianez and then leaned in. "So that's how they're different to witches, is it? They have to have a magical familiar?"

"That's right." Adianez shook her hair out. "Do you remember any birds near him?"

I frowned and then shook my head. "No, there's no way. I'd have noticed if there was a bird in his shop."

"So, he must have found a way, something to trade with in order to gain power."

I breathed out slowly. I tried to imagine myself in the tailor's shoes, and how desperate I'd have had to be to trade for power. "Did he sell his soul?"

Adianez shrugged. "Sometimes it's life force, sometimes it's the soul, sometimes it's other things, as I understand, it depends greatly on what the thing you are bargaining with wants."

I looked at Oliver, who looked rather revolted, but fascinated at the same time. "So, it could have been a demon or a spirit of some kind?" Oliver asked.

"Could be, there are all manner of things that will give power to a person willing to trade, but the most common is a fae spirit, although there are precious few of them left in our realm. Or the things you might call demons, wild beings of magic. I've heard tell of a person who bound themself to a merfolk for the same purpose, although I cannot imagine that went well."

"It's truly fascinating," Oliver said. Adianez eyed him dubiously and then dug in her pocket. She handed me a small bottle filled with a strangely pink substance.

"Here, this is the best I could do on my own. There's an amethyst in there, and my own concoction. It won't be as powerful as the last one of course, but it's solid, and should last a while."

"Thank you so much," I said, taking the bottle. I stuffed it into my shirt pocket. "Really, how can I repay you?"

Adianez shook her head. "No payment. My money's on you for destroying this damn cult, and now there's a sorcerer involved as well. Take care of them, and I'll be happy."

"If you're sure."

She smiled as she stood up from the table and sighed. "There's little I'm sure of, Cedric. Take care of yourself, and watch your back. Good luck to you, Cedric, the stars know you need it. I'll be off, if you need anything else, Dante knows where to find me."

"Thank you so much," I said, meaning it. I stroked my fingers over the small bottle and smiled at her. "For everything."

She swept out of the inn, her dress swirling impressively and I found I'd been holding my breath as I watched her go. I took a deep breath and turned to Oliver.

"Learning a lot, aren't we?"

"Indeed." He had pulled out a notebook and was scribbling in it with a pencil. I didn't recognise this one, it had a fine linen look cover in pale sky blue.

"Did you buy yourself a new notebook while you were out?"

Oliver looked up. His glasses were grubby and I was tempted to remove them and give them a clean on my shirt, but I knew he had a special cloth for it, so I resisted. "Yes, the other ones I brought are all full. There's so much to keep track of, and to record. I'm halfway through a report on Merfolk behaviour."

"Do you ever stop, I don't know, observing?" I asked, embarrassed by how much the idea of Oliver sitting and writing in his journal made me love him even more.

"Never, if I can help it." Oliver said. "I... I also have some notes about the nature and function of cursed tattoos, as well..."

"Lord, save me," I laughed.

"So," Gabriel said, striding in like a breath of fresh air. He sat beside me and put his arm around my shoulders, pulling me close to him. "I just learned something very interesting indeed."

"You did?"

"Mm. Are you finished here?" I looked at the mostly completed sketch of Mister Phillips and nodded. "Yeah, well, we know who the sorcerer is now. I'll fill you in if you like."

Gabriel let go of me and sat back in the chair. "Before you tell me about this sorcerer, I have some news too. The crew of the Purple Swan have heard of a large and fancy to do in Kingston," he said.

"Is that so?" I smiled, watching his face. "At the governor's place is it?"

Gabriel shook his head. "Oh, nothing so official. No, the rumour has it it's more along the lines of a Hellfire Club party. It's in a few weeks, under the light of the full moon in September."

Oliver leaned forward on the table and spoke in a low voice. "That sounds like a trap."

"Oh, it's certainly a trap," Gabriel said. "The cult know of Cedric's proclivities and how much he'd like a party like that, and on top of that, it's just the kind of thing that would tempt me to go out as Sir Gabriel Durant and help myself to some jewels and diamonds off the aristocracy as they let their hair down."

"Well, good," Oliver said. He swallowed. "Then we know to avoid Kingston in September."

"But it's such a well-crafted trap," Gabriel continued, as if Oliver hadn't spoken. "It begs the question who would be setting it up, and why in Kingston? And why spread the word so far and wide that you're bound to attract pirates and opportunistic thieves from all over the Caribbean?"

"It doesn't exactly sound like the cult's way," I said, slowly. "I mean, the invite to the party I went to was dashed hard to come by. Hardly anyone knew, and it was deliberately on the same night as the Governor's ball."

"And if it's not being held by the cult, who is it held by?" Gabriel said. His blue eyes sparkled with the promise of adventure.

Oliver pursed his lips and shook his head. "If we know it's a trap we shouldn't spring it. It didn't exactly go perfectly in St Vincent, after all, and we did make a plan for that."

Gabriel made a 'hmmm' noise and tapped his fingers on the wooden tabletop. "My hope is that this event is so busy with those looking to make a few ducats, that we could pass in relatively stealthily. It might require some disguises, or similar, but I think it could be worth it. Perhaps it's linked to this sorcerer."

He finally seemed to notice my sketch. "Is this him?"

"Yeah, he was my tailor, back in Kingston," I said.

"Kingston, seems like an awfully big coincidence," Gabriel said.

Oliver pinched the bridge of his nose and closed his eyes as if he'd got a sudden headache. "Well, I can't say I think it's a good idea, but I suppose you're the Captain and I can't exactly argue..."

I reached over to take his other hand and squeezed it. "We can do a lot of planning, extra good planning. And besides, the idea of you attending a Hellfire club party is just too scrumptious to pass up."

Gabriel cleared his throat and I hastily added. "Not that it's my decision either..."

CHAPTER 16

IN WHICH THE DEVIL'S WHORE CASTS OFF FROM TORTUGA

The Devil's Whore was well stocked. The recent good fortune as regards to the number of ships taken had resulted in extra groceries, and the store room was lined with salamis, smoked meats, fine looking fresh fruits and vegetables, and a huge side of pork.

I was down there hanging around Dante, since I hadn't seen enough of him in Tortuga. He was checking off all the supplies against an order sheet.

"How many sacks of flour are you sitting on, sunshine?" he asked.

I quickly hopped off the stack of sacks, and counted them. "Four. No, six. This is jolly boring, by the way."

"Yes, well, it's best we check we got everything we paid for before we cast off," Dante said. "And you didn't have to join me."

"I wanted to see you," I said. I climbed back up on the stack of flour. "And besides, you haven't fed off me in days, I expect you're positively starved."

"I did find alternatives in Tortuga," Dante said, without looking up.

My stomach did an unpleasant turn and I frowned and regarded my hands.

I'm not at all sure I like the idea of him biting other people. It's so sensual.

"And besides, I wanted to give your body some time to recover," he said. He'd crossed the room silently, and I looked up into his eyes, just a few inches from mine. My breath caught. Even though we'd been talking about his feeding, I sometimes forgot he was a predator, capable of walking on silent feet and far faster than an ordinary human could. His hand found my cheek and his thumb gently rubbed my cheekbone. "It's not good to be fed off all the time, you'd get weak and sick."

"I suppose," I said. "But I still don't like the thought of you just going around and biting people all sexy like without me."

"I don't do it all sexy like, as you so elegantly put it, with other people," Dante said. He smiled, indulgent and just for me. Leaned in and brushed his lips against the corner of my mouth like the massive tease he was. "But it's sweet of you to be jealous."

"I'm not jealous," I said, realising that of course that was exactly what I was. Dante was *my* vampire, and I wanted him biting *me. And maybe Gabriel. And, oh, how delightful it would be if he'd bite Oliver?*

My cock stiffened and I turned my head, catching his lips with mine and kissing him warmly.

Dante put his arm around me and pressed closer, and it felt like things were about to get very interesting, but then there were footsteps in the corridor and Marco appeared. Dante sprang back from me and I sat back on my hands, making no effort to hide the swelling in my trousers.

Marco's eyes dropped right to it and then back up. "Dante, have you finished your inventory? We're in danger of losing the tide."

Dante cleared his throat and picked up the discarded clipboard. "Yes, it's all good. Fine to cast off."

"Great." Marco winked at me and then scampered away.

"You're incorrigible," Dante said. He smiled at me and made a shooing gesture with his hand. "We can finish this later. I have work to do."

"Fine," I slid down from the flour sacks and kissed him softly on the mouth. "Just call me sunshine again and I'll go."

"You're my sunshine," he said. His eyes went all crinkly and adorable and I kissed him again, groaned and let go.

"All right, but I'm spending the night with you, all right?"

"Looking forward to it."

CHAPTER 17

IN WHICH THE DEVIL'S WHORE COMES UNDER ATTACK

*W*e were a few hours out from Tortuga, headed for Kingston, because Gabriel couldn't resist the lure of the trap. There was a shout from in the crow's nest.

"Alert the Captain!"

I had been sitting on the deck with my sketchpad, doing quick studies of the crew as they worked, but everyone stopped and looked up. Kaito was in the nest, and he was pointing down, towards the water.

"Something in the water!"

Scratch, who had been mending a frayed rope nearby where I was seated, got to their feet and looked into the water where Kaito was pointing.

"What is it?" Gabriel came out of his cabin at a light jog, his fingers were smeared with ink and he blinked in the sudden sunlight. He must have been doing the ship's log or something similar.

"Looks like a monster," Scratch said, turning back to look at Gabriel. The crew hadn't been making noise, but now they went extra silent. I felt my cheeks burn and hoped very very hard that the sudden appearance of a sea monster had nothing to do with me or the curse on my back.

"A monster?" Gabriel strode to the side of the ship and looked. I got up and looked as well, and sure enough, a few leagues away was a large, dark purple shape, under the water. It was coming towards us.

"Could be a whale?" Gabriel said, uncertainly. I looked at him and he was looking at Scratch, who shook their head.

"I don't think so, Captain. How about I go into the water and scout it out?"

"I think that would be best," Gabriel said. He turned back to the crew and raised his voice. "Scratch is going into the water, the thing, whatever it is, may just pass us by! But just in case, secure anything loose and prepare to defend the ship."

Scratch tore off their clothes and dove into the water. As they hit the surface their legs transformed into a magnificent tail.

Dante had been at the helm, and he passed it off to Marco and jogged down to Gabriel's side. "What do you need from me, Captain?"

"Bring my sword, will you?" Gabriel turned back to the railings and gripped them. Dante rushed off and was back in a moment with Gabriel's sword. I cleared my throat.

"Is this the kind of thing that happens often?"

Gabriel glanced at me, his expression steely. "No, Cedric. Sightings of sea monsters are rare, and they certainly have never approached my ship before."

I looked back out at the shape, which did seem to be making a beeline for us. The ocean's surface was curiously still but the thing seemed very close to the surface. Before it, a school of fish started to jump into the air, breaking the water to escape the thing.

"You wouldn't get that behaviour if it was a whale," Oliver said. I wasn't sure when he'd joined us. My heart was thumping steadily, hard enough that I could hear it echoing in my ears.

"Scratch may've put themselves in danger," Gabriel said.

"I could go in, too?" Marco said from nearby. I couldn't tear my eyes from the shape. The purple colour got darker.

"No, stay back here," Gabriel said.

There was a shout from the water. Scratch had returned, and was waving for a hand out. Marco threw a rope over the edge of the ship and Scratch hauled themselves up on it.

"Big damn lizard thing," Scratch said. They were panting hard and I'd never seen the huge merfolk look as rattled as they did now. "I've never seen one, only heard legends. My kind call it uh," they paused and thought for a moment then said a word in mermish that sounded difficult to replicate in English.

"A lizard? That large?" Gabriel shook his head.

It was closer still, perhaps a mile and a half away, when it broke the surface. My heart felt like it would stop. The huge snout of something crocodilian broke the surface and I saw the huge green eye with the cat-like slit pupil. It eyed the ship and then sunk back below the surface. The shape got smaller as it dove.

"It's going under the ship, brace yourself in case it's trying to tip us!" Scratch cried.

"Everyone brace yourselves!" Gabriel roared. He pulled me against him and braced with both hands on the railing of the ship. I gripped the railing with one hand, but reached for Oliver with the other.

I glanced sideways but Oliver was gone. I turned, trying to see him, and saw that Dante, Marco, Oliver and Bilal were lashing themselves to the main mast with rope. Under almost any other circumstances I'd have been utterly distracted with how arousing that was. But Gabriel was pressing me against the side of the ship hard enough to be painful, so I wrapped both hands around the railing and held on.

It felt as if no one on the ship breathed as the thing dived below us. Then there was a deep, low creaking noise and the deck listed to one side. I was staring at the ocean as we rose further away from it. My back pressed against Gabriel, and I felt my feet slip, or they would have, except he was holding on so tight. Our knuckles went white and then the ocean came rushing up as the ship righted itself again.

A loud scraping noise sounded from the far side of the ship, and the deck tilted the other way. This time Gabriel's weight pressed onto me and I watched with horror as the water's surface came closer.

The deck rocked back and we were upright again. Gabriel let go with one hand and shouted again.

"Kaito! What's it doing?"

"Looks like it's coming around for another pass," was the response.

"The cannons!" Gabriel shouted. "See if we can't slow it down!"

Four men rushed to the cannons and started readying them. Oliver was struggling out of the safety rope and heading towards me and Gabriel. "We're going to need something better than the cannons, I think, Captain," he said. "That looks like a plesiosaur to me. But there's never been remains of those bigger than three metres!"

"What did you just say?" Gabriel asked, softly.

"Uh, a plesiosaur, a dinosaur. If I'm right it's hide will be hard to get through, they're massive reptiles, think like a crocodile, and if it's survived this long..."

Gabriel's face had paled, but he let go of me and went to the men on the cannons, getting them ready to fire.

I swallowed. "Oliver, would... would m power work? The lightning and the light? I mean, I know I'm not meant to use my powers, but this is something of an extenuating circumstance, don't you think?"

Oliver had his hand up to his face and was furiously chewing on a nail. "The magic nature of it might be a boon, but we simply..." he looked at me, a spark in his eye and a sudden smile on his face. "We simply won't know unless we try. Come on." He took me by the wrist and dragged me to the other side of the ship, where we could see the massive beast turning in the water about a league away. It certainly looked like it would repeat its earlier attack, but it seemed to be slow to move in the water.

"You think I should just... try and hit it?" I asked. I felt uncertain now that I'd suggested it. Oliver's enthusiasm was endearing but it was a little frightening as well. Suddenly he seemed almost happy despite our situation. Energised by a scientific possibility...

"What do you need to do?" Oliver asked. He rubbed my back with an uncertain hand.

I swallowed. "Um. Usually it just happens when someone's trying to kill me, I suppose," I said. I looked at my hands.

"Well, that thing is trying to kill all of us. Look at it, and feel... whatever it is you need to feel." He pointed out to sea and I followed his gaze to see the sea monster, gaining speed. The dark shape of it seemed even larger somehow.

I raised my hands, feeling my back prickle and itch as my tattoo began to respond to... I don't know what exactly, the imminent danger, or the racing of my heart? My blood moving extra fast through my veins?

It was going to work. I gritted my teeth and *pushed* the power out. It worked beautifully. The power arced out of me like a bolt of lightning and struck the water just where the thing was. It twisted in the water, ruining its path towards the Devil's Whore.

It was definitely still moving, but it turned side on, surfacing, and its massive tail came towards the ship. Kaito shouted "brace!" from above, and I quickly grabbed the ship's rail and Oliver's hand. The ship rocked and there was a disturbing crunching noise. The deck shuddered under my feet and my back prickled, the tattoo seemed to want to fight back again.

I gasped, trying to try and tamp the prickling sensation down so I didn't hurt Oliver, who was holding tight to my hand.

"Is the hull breached?" Gabriel called. I heard footsteps, and realised I'd closed my eyes at some point. I opened them to see Marco leaning over the side of the ship.

"Cracked, but not a hole!" He responded. He righted himself. "I'll go below and see if there's anything I can do down there."

Gabriel turned to the men on the cannon. "Fire as soon as you can for fuck's sake!"

Pilcher shouted at the other two men and one of them crammed a cannon ball into the muzzle. Pilcher struck a light and lit the wick.

The monster seemed to still be regrouping and the cannonball, through some incredible stroke of luck, hit it as it was lifting its head out of the water to regard the ship. The ball struck it in the side of the neck and it flinched, recoiling with a loud, guttural roar of pain or annoyance.

Its tail flicked again, and the ship rocked.

"Again!" Gabriel shouted. "Anyone who is able, man the cannons!"

"It's not even bleeding," Oliver muttered. He let go of my hand and leaned over the railing, trying to see the monstrosity even closer. "We have to be smarter about this..."

CHAPTER 18

"Smarter?" I cried.

"Yes, it didn't like it when you hit it with your powers, it didn't like the cannonball, but I don't think either of those will stop it's attacks for long. It's not acting the way an animal who knows it's beaten would."

"So what do you suggest then?" I couldn't tear my eyes from the thing. The thrashing had created choppy waves all around the ship, which was rocking badly enough to make me seasick, if I hadn't been utterly riveted by the monster itself.

"If you could blast it again, but with a stronger force," Oliver said. It sounded like he was working it out as he spoke. "Something more powerful... and in a more sensitive spot, perhaps the inside of its mouth, or the underside of the chin, those are generally weaker places. If you could hit it in the eye, maybe... but that's a smaller target."

"I don't really control how much power comes out," I said. I raised my voice to be sure he'd hear me, because between the thrashing of the monster, people on deck rushing to the cannons and orders being shouted it had got very loud.

I glanced around and saw Dante beside Gabriel, both talking at once, and very animatedly.

"That's fine, the blast you made just needs to be intensified or enhanced..."

My skin chilled.

I thought it was too dangerous to use this power, and now Oliver's trying to work out how to make it more intense?

Still, giant sea monsters do seem to change one's perspective on things.

` "If we had something to sort of aim it, channel the power towards it like an arrow," Oliver said, his hair flicking as he whipped his head around. "If we had something long and thin like a rod, or a..." his eyes fixed on Gabriel's sword, hanging from his hip all but useless.

"He'd never let you use it," I said. But Oliver was already dashing across the deck and I was following him. He skidded to a halt, as the deck was rather wet from spray.

"Your sword," Oliver said. "Is it the biggest on the ship?"

I almost couldn't let that joke go, but at that moment the monster dove again and the ship listed hard to the side. I would have lost my footing, but Dante's arm caught me and held me against him.

"Thanks."

"Of course," Dante said. He turned back to Gabriel, who had one hand on the railing but otherwise appeared to be standing in much the same place. Oliver had grabbed hold of a barrel and was clinging to it.

"We have to take evasive action, Gabriel, please!" Dante shouted over the noise of the men racing to the other side of the ship to ready the cannons there.

Gabriel shook his head. "It's too late, and besides the thing came right for us, didn't it? It will just follow if we try and sail off. Our best bet is to kill it, or die trying."

My blood went cold. Of course, I was aware the giant sea monster could kill us, but part of me was confident that whatever happened, we'd make it out alive. Foolish of me, really.

But Gabriel's words brought home the seriousness of the situation and all thoughts of jokes vanished from my head.

"Your sword, Captain!" Oliver said again.

Gabriel looked at him in utter bewilderment. "I hardly think my sword will have much of an effect here."

Oliver let go of the barrel and shoved his hair back from his forehead, where it threatened to stick. "I have a theory that we could use it to aim the power Cedric can produce from the tattoo. If we can direct a powerful blast directly into a weak spot, it's my hypothesis that it might kill it or at least stun it so we can get away."

Gabriel inhaled, he was uncertain, I could see it in his eyes. But as the ship rocked and there was another ominous crunching sound, Gabriel shook the indecision away.

"Fuck, it's worth a try." He unsheathed his sword and handed it to me. Oliver clapped his hands once and hurried towards the back of the ship, where the sea monster was moving.

Gabriel's sword was heavy, so I used both hands to carry it, lifting it high so the tip didn't drag on the ground. I followed Oliver as quickly as I could. Behind me Dante followed, calling out.

"Wait, is it safe for Cedric to send his power through the sword? It will burn him won't it?"

"I don't know," Oliver shouted over his shoulder. "He has never been hurt before with his power, the lighting is magic, I expect it won't hurt him any more than the tattoo already does."

"It doesn't hurt to use!" I added. "It's just a bit uncomfortable!"

At the stern of the ship, Oliver turned back to me and gestured for me to stand right up against the railings. "I'll brace you."

"Hold on," Dante said. "Let me hold the sword, and Cedric can concentrate on channelling the power through it."

"But it will definitely burn you," Oliver said. His glasses were wet with salt spray but he didn't seem to notice. He frowned deeply. "It might be all right for Cedric, the tattoo might be working as protection, but you don't have the same protection."

"I will wield my sword," Gabriel said. He took it off me. "It's my ship, my crew we are defending, and it's my duty to take the most dangerous part."

"Don't be an arse," I said. I reached out to take the sword back again but he held it out of reach.

"This is my duty," Gabriel turned to Dante. "If I die, you're Captain. Get everyone into lifeboats and try and survive."

"I really must insist," Dante said. He drew himself up to his full height, which was almost exactly the same as Gabriel's, and held out his hand. "The crew needs you as its Captain, Gabriel. And I am a vampire, I can withstand a lot more than any of you can. It might hurt me, but I don't believe it will kill me as fast as it will kill you."

Gabriel wavered, and panic grew in my chest. I couldn't bear to lose any of them. "It's my power, I should use it!"

Gabriel's eyes had been locked on Dante's, and neither of them said a word. Slowly, Gabriel offered the sword to Dante, who took it and turned to Oliver. "Where should I aim it?"

Oliver swallowed, he'd been watching the monster, but had turned back just in time to see the sword change hands for the last time. "Inside the mouth, or at the eye," he said, his voice cracking. "Mouth is an easier target, since it seems to be..."

He didn't need to elaborate. We all looked to see that the monster had more or less stopped moving. It's nose was almost to the stern of the ship. Just below the surface, the massive body floated, its eyes above the water, watching us with a terrible intelligence. It was clear what its intentions would be as the snout slowly began to rise over the water. It dripped seawater and bits of seaweed as the creature opened its mouth wide enough to swallow the ship.

"It's now or never!" Oliver shouted.

Nimbly as a cat, Dante slipped over the rails to stand on the tiny ledge on the back of the ship, one hand on the railing as he leaned out, his other hand leveling the sword down the maw of the great beast.

Oliver gripped me by the hips, maneuvering me into position behind Dante.

Fuck I hope this works, or we're all royally fucked. And not in the fun way.

I could feel salt spray dripping down my face, or perhaps it was cold sweat, or even tears. I ignored that feeling and focused instead on the uncomfortable prickling in my tattoo. There must be something I could do to make it the most powerful blast I'd ever managed.

I'm about to die, I'm about to die!

I don't want to die!

The prickling shot through my veins, and I felt set alight with it, incandescent as the centre of a fire. I raised both palms towards the pommel of Gabriel's sword, leaving a few inches between me and it.

Someone shoved my shoulder as the power built and flowed to my hands, and my palms collided with the pommel at the same moment the eldritch power released.

There was a bright magnesium phosphorescent light and I felt as if I were alight with the power of angels. A burning, certainly, but not pain, not danger, only beautiful brilliant power. I didn't feel consumed by it, no. I was in control. And I let all the beautiful power flow out of me and into Gabriel's sword. The light was almost too bright to look at, and I heard, distantly, a laugh of triumph that might have been mine. It felt *good* and *right*, and resonating in my head was the echo of a word, which I had no idea why I'd ever disliked the sound of it.

Azathoth

Azathoth

Azathoth!

The light went through the sword and arced from the tip of it into the monster's mouth, deep into its throat, which I could see clearly since it was alarmingly close and open.

I was distantly aware of shouts and screams behind me. Of someone's arms wrapping around my waist, anchoring me? I didn't want to be anchored. I wanted to exalt in this new power, and embrace it fully into myself.

Dante's hand was shaking, I could feel it through the palms of my hands. I closed my fingers around the pommel to hold it straight.

Then there was a great roar, a huge echoing bellow from the belly of the beast and I saw my powers had worked. The mouth snapped shut, but short of the ship.

Dante's hold on the sword wavered, and I took it from him, held it aloft.

"Cedric!" Someone was shouting. It barely registered, as I let the remaining power within me flow through the sword and into the air.

Nothing could stop me now!

Someone slapped me across the face, and I realised there were two voices calling my name. One was Oliver.

I loved Oliver.

The other was Gabriel, who I also loved but could never bring myself to say so.

"Cedric, listen to me, come back to me. Listen to my voice and...That's it. Good boy."

I blinked, my vision suddenly clearing to see Dante, barely hanging onto the ship's railings. His fingers were slipping off the railing.

I dropped the sword and tried to grab at him, there were arms around me, holding me back. Oliver's voice in my ear. But Gabriel was there. Gabriel had both hands around one of Dante's arms but he couldn't pull him up alone.

"Dante," I said, my voice hurt to use, my throat felt scratched and raw.

Scratch appeared by Gabriel's side, and the two of them hauled him back onto the deck of the ship. I blinked again, slowly coming back to each of my senses. The smell of gunpowder, the smell of cooked meat acrid and sweet, blood. I could smell blood.

"He's right here," Oliver said. He turned me to look into my eyes. "Are you?"

I didn't understand his question, so I shook my head. "I'm fine. Let me…"

Oliver let go and I went to Dante's side. His eyes were closed, and his body limp. Scratch had stepped back, and was frowning down at the body, because that's what it appeared to be, a body. Not Dante at all, for there were no signs of life.

CHAPTER 19

IN WHICH REPAIRS ARE MADE

*H*is hands were blackened as if he'd been holding them in a fire. His normally pale skin was sickly and almost translucent, blue tinged his lips. Gabriel was pulling his shirt open and tipping his chin, as if he thought Dante needed air, or had taken in water.

A huge lump formed in my throat and my eyes teared up. "No, Dante, no…"

"He needs blood," Gabriel said.

"Will that work?" Oliver asked. "He must've taken a lot of burn damage from that last…" he trailed off. I looked over my shoulder at him, and he was looking at me with something like fear on his face.

I can't deal with that right now.

"Yes, it will restore him. I've seen him recover from wounds before with a bit of blood, although nothing like this."

"I suppose that makes sense."

Gabriel pulled one of Dante's daggers off his belt and held out his arm, about to cut himself but I held up my hand. "Wait, stop, it should be me."

Gabriel froze when I lifted my hand and I quickly lowered it again. "I just mean, it's my fault, I hurt him, he should drink from me."

"He'll probably need blood from several of us to come back," Gabriel replied. In a business-like way he sliced his own forearm with the knife, and quickly placed it to Dante's lips. "I've never seen him this bad, though."

My throat threatened to close up over the size of the lump in it. I sank to my knees beside them and picked up Dante's hand. It was always cool, but now it was as cold as the grave.

I can't lose him, I can't, I can't.

I've killed him is what I've done.

Oliver had knelt as well, and with one hand he gently lowered Dante's jaw, so Gabriel's blood would easily drip into his mouth.

I hiccuped, and then realised it was a sob. Tears were streaming down my cheeks and dripping onto my shirt. I leaned in, trying to see any kind of response from Dante, but there was nothing.

"Maybe Cedric should try," Oliver said, after a long few moments. "He has that magic in his blood, perhaps it will, I don't know, shock him back to life or similar."

Gabriel tugged a handkerchief out of his pocket and withdrew his arm. He wiped the knife off on it, then handed the blade to me. He pressed the cloth to his forearm, trying to staunch the flow of blood.

For a moment, as I held the knife, I wasn't sure I could cut myself. But my eyes rested on Dante's face, and I knew I had to try everything I possibly could to try and save him.

I swallowed, sliced my arm with a little less precision than Gabriel had done and pressed it to Dante's slack lips.

"Come on, Dante," I said, through clenched teeth. I felt my tattoo prickle again, but tried to shove that sensation back. "Come on, I need you to take the blood and wake up. You fucking bastard, you can't just die. Not like this. Not ever."

I'm not sure what else I said, but I carried on like that for a while, watching my blood dripping into his mouth.

Until I felt a slight movement. Dante's tongue, flicking weakly at my skin. I pressed my arm more firmly to his mouth. "Yes, that's it, drink," I said, my voice a little brighter. Relief flooded through me, bright as sunshine.

Oliver's hand moved away as Dante's jaw worked and finally he sank his fangs into my skin. I could feel him properly drinking now, although his eyes hadn't opened. "It's working." I turned to Oliver and smiled. "He's feeding."

"That's good," Gabriel said.

I became aware that something about this bite was different to normal though. Usually Dante's fangs penetrated my skin slowly, sensually, and his feeding felt wonderful, orgasmic even. This hurt, ached, as if I could feel every bit of blood he was pulling out of me. I groaned a little from the pain.

"Are you all right?" Gabriel asked. His face was almost as pale as Dante's. I shook my head.

"It just hurts a bit. I'll be fine."

"The way he's feeding... I don't think he's conscious yet, so it could be an instinctive reaction," Oliver said. His voice was strained still. "We might have to intervene before he drains you."

I shook my head. "He needs me, it's all right."

"It's not that simple, Cedric, he might kill you without meaning to."

"Well," I said, feeling slightly light headed. "Then we'd be even wouldn't we? I nearly killed him just now." a laugh bubbled out of my throat, alarming all three of us.

Oliver and Gabriel eyed each other, and Gabriel moved around, settling on his knees directly behind me. He wrapped his arms around my waist and I became aware of the loud sound of thumping in my ears. It was hard to hear anything else.

I wanted to lean back against Gabriel's chest, but Dante's

fangs were tearing into my arm, holding me in place. I gasped, seeing spots dancing in front of my eyes.

"Can you hear that?" I breathed, genuinely wondering.

"Oliver, we have to act now," Gabriel ordered.

Oliver used both hands, positioned them at the jaw joint, close to Dante's earlobes. "I'll try and force his jaw open. Be ready to pull Cedric back."

My arm was hurting properly now, and my heart thundering in my ears scared me. It was like it was trying desperately not to give up. Trying to keep me alive, even if my own actions wouldn't.

I closed my eyes, hardly had a choice in it, really, I was feeling so woozy.

I heard Gabriel and Oliver say things, and then Dante's teeth were gone from my arm. I pulled my arm against my chest, cradling it there. I was so sleepy, I thought I could probably go right to sleep, in Gabriel's arms where I should be.

Someone slapped my face and my eyes snapped open. Oliver was leaning over Dante's prone body, staring into my eyes, one hand pressed to his chest although I wasn't sure it'd help if he woke and wanted to feed again.

"There you are. Gabriel, we need to get food and water into Cedric as fast as we can, then it'll be all right for him to sleep."

Gabriel scooped me up against his chest and stood, carrying me away. I thought I saw movement, Dante sitting up, but there were still spots, black and silver, obscuring my vision.

Gabriel shouted orders, took me to his cabin and sat me on the bed. I think he'd ordered someone to fix the sails up and get moving. Maybe another of the orders was for food to be brought up.

Once I saw the slices of buttered bread, I felt ravenous, and each bite made me feel a little less like my mind was floating in space and a little more like myself.

I downed a half bottle of water, four slices of bread and a

chicken drumstick before it became too hard to hold my eyes open.

"Sleep now, puppy," Gabriel said, uncharacteristically gently. "You're safe."

"Dante?" I asked.

"He's going to be fine. Oliver's tending to him."

With that reassurance, I fell into a deep, dreamless sleep.

CHAPTER 20

IN WHICH REFUGE IS FOUND

I woke up in Gabriel's bed with a thumping headache, a dry mouth and what felt like a gaping hole in my stomach. I sat up and grabbed the nearest thing that looked drinkable, an old wine bottle some thoughtful person had filled with water. I drank down half of it before I needed to stop for air. Then I drank a little more and set it down. My headache eased a little as the water seeped through my system.

"All right?" I startled, as I hadn't noticed anyone in the room. It was Gabriel, he was sitting at his desk and had turned to face me.

"Hungry," I said. I rubbed my forehead. "And thirsty."

"I'll get you something to eat," he said. He came over to press his cool hand against my head, which felt absolutely sublime, then kissed my hair and went. I arranged the pillows behind me, feeling not at all like I needed to get out of bed. My body felt beaten and worn through. Partially from the magic I'd used, I assumed, but more likely from the feeding Dante had taken.

Gabriel returned with some ham sandwiches and sat on the bed, handing me the plate.

"How's Dante?" I asked, taking one half of the sandwich and biting into it.

"Eat slowly, chew it all and don't rush, you might make yourself sick if you're not careful," was Gabriel's immediate reply.

I set the sandwich down again and made a show of chewing for his benefit.

"He's all right," he said. "Oliver's been tending him. He's mostly been sleeping, but every now and then he wakes to feed a little."

I swallowed, my mouth dry again and took some more water. "I suppose he has a supply of bottles, I remember he used to anyway?"

"Those are used up," Gabriel said. "Oliver has been giving some blood, and I've given a little more as well. He's got enough, he's not drinking much at a time before he goes back to sleep."

I took another bite of the sandwich and chewed it slowly. "How long have I been asleep?"

"Probably fifteen hours, all night and then a while longer."

I swallowed and nodded. "Thanks for this, it's really good."

"The ship took a fair bit of damage from the monster, so we're going to beach her and make some repairs," Gabriel said. "We should find something suitable shortly. There's one other thing you should know though..."

I looked up, he looked serious and a little uncomfortable. "What?"

"Your tattoo, it's, well, I think it's grown again" he said. I was still wearing my sweat and seaspray soaked shirt. I peeled it off and yes, there on my right bicep was a tentacle. It was as if the thing on my back was growing vines, which wound around me. I could see it coming around my left side as well, reaching under my pectoral as if it were going to touch my nipple. My left shoulder had more tattoo as well. It was spreading.

And it was almost certainly spreading because I had used its power. I wasn't at all sure what to make of that.

"I suppose it has," I said slowly. Part of me wanted to make a joke, but nothing at all funny came to mind. "I... I'll do my best not to use the magic any more. It definitely seems to be making it worse."

Gabriel nodded, took my hand and squeezed it, but didn't say anything more. His discomfort with my magic hadn't eased any, well... how could it? He gave me a quick kiss on the cheek and then went back to his desk.

"Keep resting puppy, we'll be in a safe harbour soon enough."

I finished off my sandwich and the bottle of water, relieved myself, washed my face, and then went back to bed for another snooze.

The Devil's Whore limped to the nearest island for repairs. If a ship can be said to limp, it's certainly what happened.

I felt like myself again soon enough with more rest and plenty to eat and drink. As the ship rocked in harbour and Gabriel assessed whether it really needed beaching for the repairs or not, I went to see Dante.

Oliver was napping in his cabin when I went down there, and I felt strangely nervous about seeing him again, Dante too. I felt like a lot of things had happened in the battle with the gigantic sea creature, Oliver had been afraid of me for a moment. Dante had nearly died thanks to my magic... It wasn't the same as it had been before. Or maybe I wasn't the same?

I knocked on Dante's cabin door, although it stood a few inches open, and waited for him to invite me in.

"Yes?" His voice sounded the same. Not weak or thin, just the normal Dante velvet resonance.

"It's me," I said, and let myself in. I went to the side of his bed, where he lay propped on some cushions and pale as ever, his eyes perhaps a little more sunken than normal but otherwise looking rather normal.

"Cedric," he smiled and lifted his hand to take mine, I let him, and then twined our fingers together. His skin was clear, no trace of a burn. I felt relief flood me. "It's good to see you. I did wonder when you'd be coming down for a visit."

"I was feeling a bit shy," I said. "But also I've been sleeping a lot."

"I drank too much from you," Dante said. His face darkened with guilt and what I assumed was self-reproach. He dropped his gaze. "I'm sorry."

"*I'm* sorry," I said. "I blasted you with magic until you died."

"Well, we had to beat the sea monster back somehow," he said. His mouth quirked into a smile. "For what it's worth, you're forgiven. We did what we had to do, and I didn't want Gabriel killed."

He shuffled over in bed and I sat down beside him. "I forgive you, too," I said. "You needed blood to pull through, and I'm not at all sorry you took mine."

Dante pulled my hand to his mouth and kissed the fingertips, sending little shooting tingles of pleasure down my hand and up my arm. I cleared my throat, wanting very much for there to be more kisses, but also knowing I had to show him my tattoo.

I pushed the sleeve of my shirt up to show him the new reach of the blank ink tentacle.

Well, it's most likely not ink at all, I don't think ink can stretch on its own like this.

"My tattoo grew, again." I said, as if he couldn't plainly see that for himself. "I don't really know what it means, but I've promised Gabriel not to use the magic again. After what it did to you..."

Dante eyed the tattoo and then fixed me with an intense gaze. "What do you remember of what you were doing, when you used the power of it through the sword?"

I shook my head. "I felt very powerful, like I was channeling something incredible and…" *oh yes, that name. It had thundered in my head, repeating itself.* "And the name of the God… monster from the stars was in my head."

"You were speaking in another tongue," Dante said. "You spoke the name, I think, and a few other words. Perhaps it was an incantation, or a prayer?"

"I don't remember saying anything out loud." I frowned, and tried hard to remember, but I couldn't. But I didn't think Dante would lie about that either. My skin chilled and came out in goosebumps. "Fuck."

"And when the monster fell, you blasted power into the sky," Dante said.

"Oh, I think I do remember that," I said. "I'm sorry." I felt my cheeks warm in humiliation and shame. I shouldn't have trusted this cursed power would be free to use. I should have known better.

"You don't have to apologise. Just, be very, very careful. You know the name has power."

I bit my lip and nodded. "Yes, I know that. I won't… well, I don't know that I can promise I won't use the magic again if another sea monster comes after us, but I will not use it frivolously."

Dante took both my hands and rubbed his thumbs gently over the backs of them. "I know you wouldn't do anything to purposefully endanger the ship. You might purposefully endanger yourself, but I don't think you'd do it to Oliver, or me."

I shook my head and shuffled a little closer. "I wouldn't. I wish there was some way I could use the magic to protect you all."

"You did that. That monster would have eaten us all happily, I'm sure of it." I smiled a little and leaned in to kiss his cheek.

"Thank you, you're so wonderful. When I thought I might have lost you…" I trailed off, because it felt like my throat would close up if I kept talking about that. I shook my head. "I would have done anything." I finished.

Dante let go of my hands and gathered me into his arms, holding me close. "I know. I feel the same about you, sunshine."

We did that, just sat there and held each other for a while.

CHAPTER 21

IN WHICH THE ISLAND MAKES A PLEASANT HOTEL

Gabriel deemed the Devil's Whore in need of beaching to properly address the damage to the hull. As I understood it, Marco and Pilcher had done excellent work patching up the worst of the holes, but it had been a temporary measure. We anchored in the bay of a charming little islet to prepare.

"Thankfully since we were so flush with cash in Tortuga, Marco was able to stock up on planks, nails, and suchlike." Gabriel said to me. We were both in his cabin, packing up a few necessities in preparation to camp on the island's beach for a few nights.

"What if they got wet in the breach?" I asked. "Would we have to cut down palm trees and use those?"

Gabriel chuckled. "No, we'll wash them in fresh water and let them dry. It's not ideal but it will work. But I think they were well wrapped in oils so no need to worry yourself."

He sounded very relaxed, at ease and happy in his skin, which wasn't exactly what I'd expected since we were going to be off the waters for a few days at least and the Whore up on the sand, being hammered at instead of sailing.

"You're in an awfully good mood," I said, with something of an accusatory tone.

"A few days with a straightforward repair job and an island to ourselves sounds rather nice, that's all," Gabriel said. "We might even have a party or two."

He was walking past me so I stole a kiss. He returned it with an air of indulgence and then went to the special drawers where he kept his ropes and suchlike. I grinned.

"And what, pray tell, might you need ropes for while we bask in the sun on this lovely island?" I asked, all innocence.

"Hm, I wonder." Gabriel looked me up and down before going back to selecting items and sliding them into a bag. I tried to see over his shoulder but he was blocking me with his body. "Sometimes puppies get exuberant on the beach and need to be leashed, that's all I'm thinking about."

I moaned softly and wrapped my arms around him from behind, trying to distract him into doing something with me right then, but he wouldn't be deterred. "If you're done packing you can take your bags out and row to shore," he said, laughing a little. He peeled my hand gently back from where I was teasing at the waistband of his trousers.

I took the hint and picked up the bags I had packed. "Fine, fine. But you'll need to bring my easel, I've overloaded myself.

Gabriel eyed it suspiciously. "Are you sure it's safe for you to be painting?"

I swallowed and cleared my throat. "Not entirely, but I'd like to try all the same."

He frowned but nodded. "One of us will watch you as you paint, then we'll know right away."

Feeling distinctly untrusted, I took my things out to the longboat and soon I was wading ashore, holding the bags up over my head to keep them from the water. Oliver had taken the same longboat and was by my side as we walked out of the shallows and I took a look around.

The ocean lapped at the sand, a bright aqua colour with the golden sand, which had more white qualities than bright yellow, warm beneath it. It was going to be a good few days, I could tell.

"I think I can hear birds," Oliver said, sounding far too excited.

"Let's claim a shelter before you go running off after island birds," I said.

Bilal, Marco, Scratch and Pilcher were busy putting up tents up the beach, higher than the high tide line where there were some trees to anchor rocks from. There were a half dozen of them, and more hammocks further back, waiting to be strung between the trunks of trees.

Oliver followed as I walked towards the tents. Marco grinned as we approached. "This one's the Captain's," he said, pointing at the closest one. "But one of them is set aside for young Master Stanhope if he wants it."

"Please, just call me Oliver," Oliver said, sounding a bit tired. Or perhaps frustrated was the correct term.

"Is... are you all right?" I asked, carefully.

"Yes, largely." Oliver picked out the third tent and started putting his bags inside it. There was already a bedroll laid out on the fabric floorsheet. I wondered what Gabriel had promised the crew, or bribed them with to get them to set this all up. I lingered in the doorway, watching him. He looked up, saw me looking and sighed. "I just wish they'd call me Oliver and relax around me."

"I thought they had relaxed around you."

"Well, they don't call Dante Mister Grigorias do they? Or you?"

"They'd hardly call me Mister Grigorias," I joked. Oliver didn't laugh. I twisted my lips to one side and thought it through.

From what I've seen none of them dislike Oliver, it's not about that. They call him by his last name because... yes, I have it.

"It's because they respect you, I think," I said. "They admire your intellect, and obviously, your fine arse, and it's a measure of respect. Like calling Gabriel 'Captain'."

Oliver frowned, turned and gazed into my eyes. "Do you really think so? It does sort of make me feel like an outsider."

"I don't think they mean it that way," I said. "But honestly, the best thing you could do is talk to Marco about it. He's always upfront."

Oliver nodded a little. "He's also a sea otter."

"If anything, that's a point in his favour," I said. "He was never raised in a nursery with a governess telling him what not to do, like I was."

Oliver smiled. "I suppose you're right."

"Did you think you were unpopular perhaps?" I smiled and entered the tent properly, putting myself in his space.

"Perhaps..."

"If you are it's just because the crew is jealous of you," I said, determined to make a joke out of this so Oliver would laugh and stop being so tense.

"Jealous? Of what, exactly?" He turned to look at me, his hand going to my waist and drawing me closer. *Delicious.*

"Well, you get to spend the night with me. Obviously anyone would be jealous of that." I grinned, so he'd know just how much I was mocking myself and not him. He laughed then, low and affectionate.

His arms went around me and he kissed me swiftly, his mouth finding mine with unerring precision and I wound my arms around his neck and sighed with happiness.

"Perhaps we should pull the tent flap closed?" Oliver said, when he broke the kiss. I was busy gasping for air.

"If you like," I said, reaching behind to close the tent flap without looking.

CHAPTER 22

IN WHICH OLIVER AND CEDRIC STEAL SOME TIME ALONE

O liver made a slightly frustrated noise as the flap closed. "Perhaps we ought to be helping with the repairs and such?"

I shrugged, but to make him happy I leaned back and looked out of the tent flap. There was the longboat ferrying more people and provisions to shore, and there was no sign of Gabriel. No one else appeared to be doing repair work and... yes, there was Dante, sitting on the beach, leaning back on his hands and watching as a familiar looking sea otter played in the waves. I pulled my head back in.

"No, no one else is. Looks like we have a little time we could steal."

"Well, then," Oliver said. He kissed me again, sucking on my tongue and then my bottom lip. It felt as if it had been a long time since I had been alone with Oliver, in such a way. Certainly we had spent time together on the ship, but often there had been others involved, which was not at all a bad thing but it made this time with just me and him together rather special. I'd been yearning for him, I realised.

I pulled back from the kiss to undo the buttons on his shirt and mouth my way down, kissing his nipples and then the ridges of skin over his ribcage. I sank to my knees as his fingers carded through my hair, tugging gently at the curls and I moaned my approval. He tasted salty and good, and I found myself thirsty for more of him. I tugged his trousers open and leaned in to coax his cock out and into my mouth.

I spared a glance upwards and saw Oliver tilting his head back and moaning, but biting his lip, perhaps so he didn't make too much noise. The tent walls would hardly muffle anything after all. A wicked impulse overtook me and I resolved to get him to moan so loud everyone on the beach would hear exactly what we were doing. It would be a fun challenge, perhaps.

Settling myself more comfortably between his legs I licked his cock up and down, teasing at the corded veins and at the seam of his foreskin. Oliver's hips bucked, involuntarily it seemed, and his breathing was heavy, panting over me.

His fingers twisted in my hair, tugging gently and I groaned around him, trying to transfer the vibrations of it into more teasing for him. His other hand closed on the back of my neck and I realised he was holding me in place. I knew what that indicated and my past plan to make him loud vanished out of my mind as his actions went directly to fuel my own arousal.

I let my jaw slacken and opened my eyes as I nodded as slightly as I could. Oliver's hips bucked with more purpose as I let him use my mouth. I delighted in the even more salty taste of his pre-ejaculate, and the fact of being used for his pleasure. It was demeaning, in a way, but it was in a way that my twisted body thoroughly enjoyed.

I palmed myself through my trousers and moaned again. Then Oliver's hand tightened painfully in my hair, the grip on my neck fell away and he was pulling me back off him.

"Not like this," he rasped. "Not with you touching yourself." He still had a firm grip on my hair so it hurt to nod.

"Whatever you want," I managed to reply. My own throat felt

a little raw from being used, and bereft of the satisfaction of completion. He moved back onto the makeshift bed.

With another sharp tug on my hair, and his other hand gripping my bicep he guided me on top of him. I braced myself with one hand planted on the bedroll beside his head, gazing into his eyes with a sudden and almost overwhelming rush of emotion that I could hardly name. Love, yes, and affection, but something deeper as well. A kind of understanding of who I was with him, and who he was, and how he accepted me with all my flaws and inconsistencies and, well, curses. And I knew that I too would accept whatever he threw at me. I could overlook it when he was annoying, or overly critical or prissy. Because I loved him.

The purity of my love for him was somewhat overwhelmed when his hand closed around both of our cocks and he pumped them together, velvet skin on velvet skin and the most delicious tease in the world.

"Oh, fuck, Oliver." I buried my face in his neck.

His hand released my hair finally, it stroked down my spine from the base of my skull to just above my waist. His hold was so steady, so reassuring, and I rolled my hips, using his movement as a guide.

"That's it, too hot to wait," he murmured. "Just need to come with you right now."

The idea that Oliver not only was hot enough for me that he couldn't wait to prep and properly fuck me, and more than that, he was so hot he wasn't even talking in complete sentences, had me coming fast and without warning. Oliver wasn't far behind and his hand stroked the slickness over the both of us as we kissed again. As soon as he let go of me I collapsed to the side and we both lay still, breathing loudly.

Finally I rolled towards him and kissed him gently on the nose. "I love you, Oliver."

He threw his arm around my waist and tugged me closer. "I know. I love you too, Cedric."

CHAPTER 23

IN WHICH THE CREW OF THE DEVIL'S WHORE
HAVE SOME MUCH NEEDED REVELS

few hours later, I woke up in an empty tent. I pulled my trousers on, and went out to see what was happening on the beach, not bothering to do my shirt up again.

The bonfire was built high, and the heat from it scorched my face if I got too close. The burning wood smelled good, but better than that was the smells of roasting sausages. Cook had arranged large stones at the edge of the fire to work as a kind of griddle and the scent made me salivate.

Kaito had gone into the forest and returned with large, spikey pineapple fruits, which he twisted the green leafy tops off of and sliced. They were delicious and juicy, sweet and a little tart. But the pieces he let roast on the hot stones were even more delicious.

The mood had turned very jovial, and as the crew finished eating, Pilcher pulled out a guitar and started to strum. Bilal slapped their hand on their thigh to make a rhythm and they started to sing a song about someone's one true love, lost at sea. The rest of the crew joined in and soon all who knew the words were singing.

I found the barrel of wine that had been opened and decanted some of it into a water jug to bring it to the others to fill their cups. A cheer went up around the fire as the song finished and there was a ragged round of applause.

"Thanks, puppy." Gabriel pulled me into his lap and kissed my neck, his breath fruity with wine. "We needed this, I think."

"I think so, too." I leaned back against him and looked around at the different faces, the firelight flickering over them as the sun went down. There was a certain amount of relief reflected back at me.

Dante was leaning back on his hands, his eyes on the fire and a dreamy look in his eyes. He was more or less back to his normal colouring, which was a balm to my heart. It had been a tense few nights watching him recover and Gabriel had kept him off active duty for the most part. But he looked himself again, and it warmed my heart.

Gabriel's hand stroked over my stomach and I hummed, kicking my legs a little in the sand.

"Go on, Oliver!" The call went up and Oliver stood, laughing but ducking his head, scrubbing a hand through the hair on the back of his head.

"Go on, sing us a song!"

"Oh, I love his voice," I said, loud enough for Gabriel to hear but not anyone else. "He has a lovely tone."

"Mmhm." Gabriel rested his chin on my shoulder and the two of us focused on Oliver.

Oliver took a breath and started to sing a song I'd never heard before, although a line in I thought I recognised it from somewhere.

"Under the greenwood tree
Who loves to lie with me,
And turn his merry note
Unto the sweet bird's throat, come hither, come hither..."

Oliver's voice was clear and true, and it carried over the crew. They had largely gone quiet to listen to him, but there were some titters as people realised the nature of the song. Oliver's eyes found mine and he sang directly to me for a moment, then his eyes slid to Gabriel's.

"Shakespeare, I believe," Gabriel said, after Oliver had turned his gaze again, this time to Dante.

"Yes, you're right I think. I think it's from As You Like It..."

Oliver finished up the song and everyone applauded and cheered and Oliver laughed and took a bow before flopping onto the sand beside Dante.

"Very nice," Dante said to him.

The evening wore on with mock duels between crew members including a very energetic display from Kaito and Bilal. Kaito using a long piece of driftwood as a staff and Bilal using two shorter pieces to counter. It was highly impressive.

Later there were more songs and even some dancing. I managed to drag Gabriel up into a lively polka around the fire. I was very pleased to make him loosen up even a little. Oliver tried to teach Scratch a human dance, but they didn't take to it naturally.

The wine flowed, laughter was quick and easy and it felt as if a weight had lifted off the crew. *A celebration of life, perhaps, having come so close to losing that...*

At the end of the night I went to bed with Dante, happy and tipsy.

CHAPTER 24

IN WHICH CEDRIC'S DREAM IS A LITTLE TOO CLOSE FOR COMFORT

I am high above the ground. Looking down.

I am cold and warm at the same time. It's cold out here, so high, but it's where I live and I am comfortable. There is time.

I can see so much, for so far, so much ocean. The ocean is full of ships, full of islands, full of animals and fish. The ships ferrying people between the islands and the landmasses. I can see the patterns of ocean currents, the strange lines in the water that denote where a particularly strong one moves. Or the waves where two intersect, white foam on the sparkling water.

And I can feel the leviathans below. The colossal beasts, the beings who slumbered until recently.

There is time.

The great sea beasts have never paid attention to me before, there was no way they could have. Too much distance divided us. But now there is the lever. The conduit. And his body is working for me, it is channeling some of me through into the world and the leviathans respond.

Below the surface of the water they wake, and they seek him out... and perhaps they will destroy it all and I'll be thrown back amongst the stars once more.

It is all one to me.

Either my loyal followers will succeed in using the Chosen One to bring me closer still, through into this delicious world, or they will not. I have waited this long. I can wait eons, again. I am nothing at all if not patient.

I watch as a kraken uncoils itself, achingly slowly, from its hibernation cave, deep beneath the ocean's surface. Its arms are vaster than many of the islands that dot the ocean. It will take some time to wake properly, and even more time to warm up enough to swim. But it will do it.

There is time.

On the beach I see the humans, the conduit and the ones protecting him. Some are sprawled over the sand like so much debris washed ashore, and some are under makeshift canopies, but none are hidden from my sight.

I watch the conduit - Cedric - wake with a start, shuddering with fear. He was lying on his side, his back pressed to one of the others, and his hand resting beside his face. He opened his eyes, looking for a drink to relieve the dryness in his mouth. His mouth is so dry.

In the pre-dawn light his eyes needed little time to adjust. Cedric saw that the inked tattoo of a tentacle had spread all the way to his hand. He let out a yelp of fear.

CHAPTER 25

IN WHICH DANTE OFFERS HIM SOME COMFORT

y heart pounded so hard I swear my chest was vibrating with each pulse. My mouth was so dry my tongue was sticking to my teeth but I couldn't see a bottle anywhere. I scrambled to my hands and knees and then up, bashing my head on the bamboo stake crossbeam that was supporting the tent I'd fallen asleep in and swore.

"Cedric, what's wrong?"

I felt a hand on my wrist and yelped again, because even though Dante had spoken and I'd heard him sit up I was still startled by his touch. His fingers dropped away and I shook my head. "Drink," I managed to rasp.

"Here." Dante reached behind him and handed me a glass bottle full of water. I uncorked it and drank quickly, downing a third of it before I took a breath.

The breath was rattling and shallow so I tried again, tried to calm my heart with a long slow inhale. I let it out my mouth again with a *whoosh*.

Dante reached for me again but didn't touch me, and I looked at his offered hand and then at my own. Corking the bottle again, I saw the flashes of black. I hadn't imagined it, it wasn't just some lingering night horror... the tentacle had extended itself again.

I sat down heavily on the blanket I'd been lying on because it was too hot to be under and looked at my hands as if they didn't belong to me at all.

Am I still me?

In the dream I wasn't... I could see me. I was above and I could see my body, even through the tent.

Tears welled in my eyes.

Dante was next to me, slipping his arm around me and talking low. I tried to concentrate on what he said, I knew it was important after all, but all I could hear was my own thoughts repeating.

I wasn't me. I wasn't me. I wasn't me.

"Cedric, look at me." Dante's voice was more commanding this time and it broke through into my reverie. I looked up, my vision blurring with tears. "It was another nightmare wasn't it? I can sense it... tell me what happened."

I shook my head.

I can't tell him. It's too awful. If he knew I had become... that thing... that it was so aware, so close, watching me...watching all of us. It knew about the others, and it would kill them so easily. And then the monsters!

I was shaking, my teeth rattled against each other until I clenched my jaw so tight it ached. I closed my eyes and covered my face with my hands.

Why did I ever go to that fucking party? That was the start of it all. I should have been a good boy and gone to the party at the Governor's house that night, then I wouldn't be in this predicament. I wouldn't have to deal with monsters and curses and being pursued.

I'm such a worthless idiot.

Dante pressed me tight against him and continued to murmur. I tried my best to listen to him.

"You're all right, you're safe here. I won't let anything hurt you, you know that. I'm here with you Cedric, and I love you."

It took every ounce of my strength to focus on those words. I liked those words, I knew I did, but I felt so lost. Adrift on a sea of fear and horror and self-pity.

I started to sob, which felt like more of a communication than simply clenching my teeth. After a moment of that, I thought perhaps I could say something to Dante, so I cleared my throat, and then cleared my throat again.

"I love you, too."

Dante's hand rubbed slow circles on my back, which was always a good move for comforting. It felt like either Gabriel or Dante was always having to rub circles into my back to soothe me. I felt a fresh batch of tears well from my eyes and run down my face.

"It's all right, we'll solve this, Cedric. My sunshine. We'll make you safe again, I swear it."

I wanted to believe it. I wanted to believe so hard, but I was still so lost.

"Maybe I should just, go and be on my own a bit," I said, finally. I loved Dante and I knew he meant well, but the words and actions simply weren't enough today. I needed to think.

"If that's what you need, of course. Just don't wander too far from camp, all right?"

I got up from the bed, pulled on some trousers and one of Dante's voluminous shirts, picked up my sketch book from where it sat on a folding table and went out onto the beach.

The sun was bright, and it helped a little to chase away the fear that was plaguing me. I didn't dare look up at the sky though, too fearful that I'd see something there I didn't like.

Dante's shirt was large enough on me that the sleeve came down over my hands, allowing me to conceal the way the tattoo had stretched. I would have to show Gabriel, of course, and perhaps Dante was telling him about it right now, but for the moment I didn't want to deal with it.

I walked until I couldn't hear the noises of hammering on the hull, or people talking. I could still see the crew of the Whore, further down the beach, but their figures were tiny.

I set myself up in the shade of a coconut palm, seated on the hard packed sand with my back against its smooth surface. The sand felt good between my toes, scratchy but familiar, something real that I could focus on.

What else could I focus on?

The sound of the waves lapping at the shore. Soothing and regular, every now and then a slightly larger wave. Was it every seventh wave? Was that a real thing? Someone told me that once, but why would the ocean count in sevens?

I tipped my head back and reluctantly looked up to the sky. Although part of me was afraid, I needed to know that there was nothing up there but the sun and some clouds. If there was anything watching me - if *Azathoth* was watching me, I couldn't see it. It looked the same as any other brilliant Caribbean day.

My breathing was quick, so I tried to concentrate on the feel of the sand under my feet and slow my breathing down. I had nothing to fear right this second. The thing from beyond the stars wasn't going to pop down to the beach. No one was actively trying to snatch me away.

I dropped my eyes to the horizon and scanned, but there was nothing out there. No ships of bounty hunters, no sea monsters emerging from the deep. I could relax.

I told myself that a few more times before I started to believe it.

More at ease, I opened my sketch book and started to draw. I slashed a line across the page to be the horizon, and then tried to capture the movement of the ocean on the page, an impossible task to be sure, but an amusing one. Lines could hold so much meaning if they were created right, after all.

I let myself sink into the exercise, letting the larger fear go and settling into the almost meditative practice of focusing on my art. In this state I could truly be myself.

Not that I exactly knew what that meant. I didn't know how to truly be myself beyond knowing I didn't have to please anyone in that moment. I didn't need to be aware of what others were thinking about me, or feeling, or what they wanted from me. I could simply please myself with making something beautiful.

In this frame of mind, I could feel myself relaxing, my breath slowing to an even pace and my shoulders unknotting. The tension I hadn't realised I'd been holding in my jaw eased, and the relief was exquisite.

I set my charcoal down and stretched my fingers, reaching them out and apart and that felt so good I did the same with my legs, stretching them as long as they could go and wriggling my toes.

I went back to sketching and became aware of something else. Something I'd never noticed while creating art before. Another presence.

It wasn't near me, in fact, as my heart sped up with fright, I realised it wasn't physical at all. There was another presence in my mind. There was something there, settled in the back like a toad under a stone, and it was watching me.

Moving very slowly, I set the sketchbook and the charcoal down on the sand. I should get up and go to Dante, see if he had some way of... what? Seeing into my mind? Magically banishing... whatever it was?

The witch's magic should have prevented this, shouldn't it?

I felt in my pocket for one of the crystals and my fingers closed around the smooth, cool surface. My panic eased a little.

There's nothing to worry about. I probably just imagined it, all that staring at the sky and worrying about Azathoth... maybe I shouldn't say his name even in my head, that would be like inviting him in, perhaps.

I took a deep breath, which caught a little in my throat and tipped my head back. I felt suddenly too hot, and a little dizzy. I closed my eyes and slumped back against the tree trunk, sighing out loud.

I just wanted to relax, was that too much to ask for?

I sat like that for a few minutes, finally becoming aware that my hands had picked up the book and charcoal again. I didn't remember doing that. I could hear the scratch of the point on paper, and my eyes fluttered open to see I had sketched a sea creature. Something that appeared as if it could have been human at one point, but its eyes were far too big, and its mouth a wide gash of spiked teeth.

In the picture it was emerging from the ocean, walking towards the viewer, towards me. Beyond, in the waves, which I had managed to capture some of the movement of, there were more shapes, a domed head emerging, as if there were a large group of the things.

My fingers tightened on the stick of charcoal and it splintered.

I couldn't show this to the others. But I probably should show it to the others. But if I did they'd... what? Take away all my art supplies? Maybe that wasn't such a bad idea.

I tipped my head back against the tree trunk and sighed. "Why is nothing ever easy?"

CHAPTER 26

IN WHICH TIME IS PASSED AND PLANS ARE FORMED

Gabriel took my art supplies back to the ship, as I expected. I couldn't bring myself to argue with him about it, the memory of being Azathoth and watching my own body and those of the rest of the crew were fresh in my mind, and the fear that it brought on sapped me of resistance. Besides, it was probably the right thing to do, right? It could have been a way I was inadvertently opening myself up to... the thing.

Instead of spending time alone with my increasingly alarming thoughts, I followed Oliver around as he explored the plant life of the island. It was a little dull, but his enthusiasm for noting it all down was rather delightful.

"I could try and sketch the plant for you, if you like?" I suggested at one point, when he'd found a fern he didn't think he recognised from any readings.

Oliver's face lit up for a moment, delighted, but then he realised what I was suggesting. I realised it too, a few moments too late.

"Not that I *want* to uh, tempt whatever it is that takes over my hand," I said quickly.

"Maybe it's best if you don't," Oliver said. He slipped his pencil into his breast pocket, as if to hide it from me.

I wished I could be more helpful, but instead I was a liability, that's what it felt like. It was hardly even safe for me to sleep, although I did have a delightful afternoon nap, pillowing my head on Dante's lap as he studied maps of our next course.

That night, the ship's repairs were being sealed with pitch and the captain announced we'd be sailing out the next afternoon, once the pitch had dried and the ship was back in the water, of course.

The crew were a little more reserved that night on the beach. Instead of a party there were small groups clustered here and there, and the bonfire was more of a cooking flame and not much more.

I was seated in between Dante and Oliver, which is a spot I had chosen for myself, on account of them being so good to me. However, it had started to feel a little like I'd stuck myself in between two minders, or prison wardens, as they were both being exceptionally attentive. I found myself gazing longingly at where Scratch and Marco were playing together in the waves, tossing a coconut back and forth, and being increasingly dramatic with their catches. Marco doing a backflip before catching the makeshift ball one-handed was particularly impressive.

Gabriel had been making the rounds, speaking to each of the groups of pirates before he came to sit beside Oliver and sighed.

"It's been pleasant here, hasn't it?"

"Yes, very," Oliver said.

"Depends on where you're sitting," I grumbled. Gabriel shot me a concerned look.

"Yes, your dreams, and your drawings. I think we ought to take aggressive action," he said.

"Aggressive in what way?" Dante asked.

"We're headed to Kingston, to see what we can find out at the Hellfire Club." Gabriel's eyes flicked between us, gauging our responses, perhaps waiting for an objection. "I'm aware it will most likely be a trap, but it's our best lead to find out how to undo all of this."

"Kingston is where it all started," I said. I kicked at the sand, hardly sure why I felt so pettish and belligerent.

Unless it's the thing in my head doing it? I thought, and then instantly dismissed the idea. It felt like going backwards somehow, and although I was sure it was a false fear, part of me worried that all we'd had in the last months would be undone. We'd go back to the beginning, the Devil's Whore would sail off without me, and I'd be left alone.

"I'm not sure that's a good idea," Dante said. He eyed me and I screwed my lips together so I didn't say something terrified and irrational about how I didn't want them to leave me when absolutely none of them were suggesting it.

Gabriel shrugged. "It's the only thing that makes sense."

CHAPTER 27

IN WHICH GABRIEL AND CEDRIC TALK OF
THE FUTURE AND THE PAST

The voyage back to Kingston was punctuated by one attack on a French merchant ship, in which most of the takings were wine. One case of each variety of wine was divided between the crew, and the rest sold at a trading port along the way.

"What are you planning to do with all the money?" I asked Gabriel, as we set sail again from the trading port. He had a heavy purse in his hands that he was securing in the small safe in his cabin. I was lounging provocatively on the bed dressed in only a pair of undone trousers.

"Well, a fair amount of that is the crew's pay," Gabriel said. "When we land in Kingston Dante pays them and they can all go on shore leave while we infiltrate the party."

"Right, but you get a share for yourself, as well," I said. I stroked a hand idly over my stomach, hoping he'd notice and pounce on me. "Do you have plans to retire? Purchase a Manor house in the English countryside? Plate the Devil's Whore in gold?"

Gabriel rewarded my quip with an indulgent chuckle. "I used to do this for the thrill, with the ultimate goal of buying myself a proper title and going to court." He turned away to hang up his coat as he spoke, and I watched the lines of muscles in his back tense under his shirt. His shoulders carried the weight of the past, perhaps.

"I sense a but...?"

"But everyone in court would know I purchased a title. Even now, when I attend parties as Sir Gabriel no one truly accepts me as one of the nobility. Oh, they're polite and all, of course they are, but I'm never asked to a private supper, or singled out in the way I used to want to be."

I frowned a little. Having been born to money and noble standing it was hard for me to imagine what that might feel like.

"So, your plans have changed?"

"My plans have evolved," Gabriel said. He turned back towards me, his sapphire eyes blazing with intent. "I thought I would feel sad to give up something that used to be so important to me. Instead, I welcome it. When I kidnapped you, I imagined the payment would be what I needed to move on. But you brought so much trouble to the ship..."

He didn't say the words in an accusing way at all. He said them as if he welcomed the trouble and perhaps he did. My heart was racing and not just because of the way he was looking at me, but because he'd never talked about himself to me in such detail. Never opened up about what he wanted or didn't want in life. It was terribly exciting to be let in like that.

"I did, yeah," I said, lightly. I didn't let any of the weight of my very real guilt for putting them in danger touch my tone. "I brought sunshine into your life, if you believe what Dante says."

Gabriel sat on the edge of the bed and removed his boots. "He's not wrong in that regard."

"And more than that?"

"You brought adventure," Gabriel said. "More satisfying and strange than any I'd discovered for myself simply pirating."

I went to my knees and shuffled behind him, draping my arms around his shoulders and smiling as his heat seeped into my bare chest. I nuzzled behind his ear and made him chuckle.

"So what I'm hearing is that I have vastly improved your life and you love me to bits."

Gabriel stiffened slightly and then relaxed.

I froze, realised we hadn't actually said those three words to each other yet, he and I. I swallowed, but he chuckled again.

"You give yourself an awful lot of credit, puppy," he growled in a way that sent thrills through me and specifically to my cock. His hand reached up and closed on mine where it rested on his chest. He hadn't said he *didn't* love me, so that was something. "But you're distracting me right now."

"What am I distracting you from?" I let my fingers trail over his chest and to his nipple, gently tugging on it.

"We need to plan for the Hellfire Club party," he said. "Tell me what it's normally like?"

"Well, I've only been to one. But it's probably easier to show you than describe it..." I said, slowly. I tugged on his nipple, pinching it between thumb and forefinger until his hand closed on my wrist and pulled me off him.

"Maybe just describe it in words, a detail might be lost otherwise."

"Fine. It was a masquerade, everyone wore their finest, plus a fancy mask."

"So no one knew who their partner was?"

"Well, you sometimes learn to recognise a voice, or a hairstyle," I said. Gabriel leaned back against my chest and tried to look at me. It was a strange reversal of heights but I didn't hate it.

"And was it a normal party to begin with?"

I thought back to that alcohol infused night and tried to remember. "Yes, more or less. There were footmen welcoming us in, and lots of trays of champagne. There was music and some people were dancing, although..." a memory stirred and I tried to recall if it was a true one or something I'd dreamed. "I think there were topless people right from the start. In giant ornate bird cages. Barely dressed, bare chested with skimpy little shorts and skirts on. They had masks of birds as well."

"How long before things started to change?"

I bit my lip. "I think the host opened a door, which went to a downstairs chamber. Like a big ballroom but below ground. Small, high windows on the wall, but the room was mostly below ground level, I think, I remember the morning light waking me. And down there people started doing things with ropes and whips, I think. That's where it starts to get very hazy. I remember wondering the next morning if there had been something stronger than wine in those glasses."

Gabriel frowned. "None of us will drink what is offered, this time around. I can sneak a bottle in and fill our glasses that way."

"Probably a good idea." I shuffled back against the pillows, pulling Gabriel with me and he came willingly enough, propping himself up on one elbow.

"So anyone might sleep with anyone? Is the idea behind the masks?" He asked, his hand resting open palmed on my stomach. I watched it rise and fall.

"Yes, broadly."

"Well, that won't do," he said. "I shall have to make it abundantly clear that you belong to me from the moment we step inside." His expression turned into something wicked and I feigned innocence.

"I'm sure I haven't the foggiest idea of what you're referring to, Captain..."

In one quick movement, Gabriel turned and pinned me to the bed, his teeth bared in a wolfish smile. "I think you do have an idea."

"No, nothing in my head at all," I lied. "You shall have to enlighten me."

He gathered both my wrists in one of his hands and trailed his other down the side of my throat. "Your leather collar, for a start. Maybe I'll put a leash on it, and walk you in like the disobedient puppy you are."

I shivered despite myself. "Well, I'm sure it's hardly the most shocking thing that would happen at a party like that..."

"One of those harnesses, perhaps. But maybe... hm..." He leaned in and kissed my Adam's apple and then bit the skin there. "Maybe an arm binder."

"Arm binder?" My voice cracked on the words, no doubt inspiring him to even more mischievous thoughts. "What exactly...?"

Gabriel chuckled darkly and nipped his way back up to my ear and bit the lobe. I gasped and my back arched off the bed. I was more than ready for more teasing, but I did also want him to actually do something to release the tension he was creating as well.

"Fuck, please, Captain," I gasped. I tugged against the hold he had on my wrists and his grip tightened in response.

"I don't know how we expect to learn anything at this party," he said, breathless in my ear. "I'm going to be absolutely distracted looking at you, mostly naked and ready for me."

Mostly naked? Well, all right...

"It was your idea, after all," I said, not unreasonably although my voice was rather strained.

"And Dante and Oliver, too," he murmured, as if I hadn't spoken. "The three of you are so diverting. But it must be done. Once we have the cult off your very fine tail..." he sat up, letting go of my wrists in order to strip my trousers off and flip me over. My cheek met the bedclothes and I pushed my knees under me, displaying the aforementioned tail for him. "Then I can really take my time in enjoying you."

With that he gripped my hips and dropped his face down to lick me open. It was almost more than I could bear. I was already highly aroused, by his words as much as his actions, and now his tongue was doing so much more.

I whined, trying to press back against him but his grip on my hips tightened. I imagined I would have fingerprint shaped bruises there in the morning.

He wasted no time in stretching me, adding his fingers to his tongue and soon he was slicking himself with coconut oil and pushing inside.

"Yes, oh for the love of... yes!"

I was beyond making sense, and then his hand wrapped around my throat, simulating the collar I expected he was thinking about. His grip tightened, not enough to cut off my breath, but enough to indicate he could if he wanted to.

My cock was aching, so flush with blood and need. "Please!"

He was leaning on his other hand, but he pulled himself up enough to stroke me. I lifted my hips as much as I could, encouraging him in all the ways I knew how, I could feel myself clenching around him and I wanted so much for him to achieve his ecstasy before I did.

"That's a good puppy," he said, which, as with so many things should have been more demeaning than arousing, but my body found it arousing all the same. "With me."

I closed my eyes and listened to his breathing, confident that I'd be able to pinpoint the timing, but battling with myself because I was already ready to orgasm. I bit my lip and tried to hold off, focusing all my attention on the sound of his moaning.

He came and with relief I let myself as well, both of us moaning and groaning, and my whole being feeling utterly at peace with the world.

He cleaned us both up and lay on the bed beside me, opening his arm so I could drape myself over his chest and the two of us caught our breath.

"Maybe I should wear something very concealing and

unattractive to the party," I said after a time. "Then you wouldn't be distracted."

"I can't imagine anything you could wear that would make you unattractive."

I blushed, and smiled, and hid my face in his neck. "That was far sweeter than I expected the response to be."

"Well, don't get used to it, puppy." His hand stroked my back idly and I sighed, the feeling of utter peace overwhelming me. Whatever his words, I could absolutely get used to this kind of thing.

Perhaps you're already used to it, and you're taking it for granted. It'll soon all be swept away from you.

"Ssssh," I mumbled, to the voice inside my head. And then I was asleep.

CHAPTER 28

IN WHICH THERE IS ABSOLUTELY NO CHANCE
THIS IS SIMPLY A SEXY PARTY, IS THERE?

*W*e arrived in Kingston a day and a half ahead of the party, thanks to fine winds and clear waters. This gave Gabriel and some of the more discreet members of the crew time to find out more about the party, where it was held and what to expect.

Dante returned that night with valuable intel from a local vampire.

"How do you know absolutely every vampire?" I asked him. I was in the copper tub of water, bathing when he returned to Gabriel's room. Oliver was writing a letter or in his journal or something, and Gabriel had been napping but sat up when Dante returned.

"I don't know *every* vampire," he said. He hung his impressive black cape up on the hook and turned back. "Just the ones worth knowing in most of the ports we frequent."

"*I* want to meet vampires," I grumbled.

"You know one vampire already, that's plenty," Oliver put in. The old tutor voice and lack of patience distinct.

We had hired rooms at the Rose and Crown near the docks, as cover and to distance ourselves a little from the ship if anyone were to follow. The Crew had a watch schedule to stick to, alternating staying with the ship and enjoying themselves in Kingston.

"What I learned was that the man hosting the party at his house hasn't done anything like this before," Dante said, changing the subject deftly. His name is Reginald King and he's known to frequent the tailor who used to have a store here in town, your Mister Philips, Cedric."

"He wasn't *my* Mister Philips." I bit my lip and looked down. "So you're saying they're working together to lure us in?"

"Sounds like it," Dante sighed, but then his countenance brightened. "But the good news is that several of my friends will be there. Keeping an eye on things, as it were."

I sat up and some of the water sloshed out of the tub with my sudden movement. "So I can meet more vampires?"

"The less attention you bring to yourself or to Dante's friends, the better," Gabriel said.

"Maybe afterwards," Dante said. He crossed the room and kissed me on the forehead before going to sit on the bed.

The rest of the night we made more careful plans, including who would be wearing what, and went to sleep early at Oliver's insistence, to preserve our energy.

The day was largely resting and eating, going over the plans again and finally, finally it was time to prepare.

As promised, or perhaps I more rightly should say threatened, Gabriel dressed me in fitted black silk breeches that ended just under the knee, a heavy leather collar with a large ring on the front of it and little else. No arm binder eventuated, which some part of me was disappointed about, but he did have some little leather straps that fastened around my wrists and biceps. They had rings on them like the collar, as if at any time I *could* be bound with them, but functionally they were like very fitted bracelets.

"Is it all right for me to go with no shirt with my tattoo out like this?" I asked, turning this way and that to examine myself in the looking glass.

"Ideally we'd conceal everything about who we are," Dante said. "But as we are trying to find out as much as we can perhaps this will expedite matters."

Gabriel cleared his throat, looking at me and then Dante. "Yes, it should work to our advantage, letting the cultists come to us."

"I'm not entirely comfortable with using Cedric as bait," Oliver said, frowning.

"We will all have our eyes on him," Gabriel said. He was in fact, looking at me very closely, somewhat lustfully.

Dante, for his part, wore a black and grey tartan kilt, with a leather harness over his white shirt, it looked divine, and I wanted very much to grab it and pull him in for kiss after kiss, but our goal was to get to the party, not be sidelined with having fun with each other.

Gabriel had dressed in his signature black Lucifer garb, and as ever, it made him seem about a foot taller.

Oliver had struggled a little with what to wear, as his clothing was all very ordinary and proper, but between the three of us we had managed to put together something that made him look a little more sinister, more like a dominant and mysterious sort of man. His own deep grey shirt, a black waistcoat from Dante, black trousers and a fitted frock coat in midnight blue. It took nearly all my willpower not to pounce on him and tear it all off.

I had a slug of whiskey before we left, just to calm my nerves.

"That's all you're drinking tonight, Cedric," Gabriel said. "Unless it's from the bottle of water I've got in my coat."

"Yes, Sir," I said. I thought back to the Cedric of so many months ago, preparing for his first attendance at the Hellfire Club. I had downed most of a bottle of wine before even leaving the house. I was untroubled then. It felt like a lifetime ago, or at least a few years. That Cedric had been carefree, worrying about nothing at all past where the next drink or the next fuck was coming from. I felt immeasurably older than him, now.

I shrugged on a coat for travelling and we made our way out of the inn and through the streets to the Manor house in a hired carriage.

As we stepped out of the carriage, we left our coats and outerwear inside, in order to look appropriately debauched and ready for whatever was inside. The party wasn't explicitly a masquerade so Gabriel had decided we wouldn't wear masks. They might make us stand out a little too much if not many others were wearing them.

The house itself was a large, imposing English tudor style mansion with lights in every window. It was surrounded though, not with a carefully tended lawn, but many tall tropical trees. Presumably for privacy, although I had thought this was the first such party that had been hosted here. There were many carriages parked outside, and although it already seemed busy inside there were still people arriving as we had.

Inside the place was a swirl of colour and flesh. More people present than I would have believed possible for a Kingston party, but then again the word of the event had traveled far and wide.

"Oh, Heaven preserve us," Oliver muttered softly. I caught Dante's flinch out of the corner of my eye.

"Mind your language," I said, briskly. "This is clearly Hell if it's anywhere."

Gabriel tugged on the leash clipped to my collar. "Quiet puppy," he said. I flushed and bit my lower lip.

Oliver gave me a hungry look, his eyes on my throat and then my bare chest.

I squared my shoulders, glanced at my arms, adorned as they were with leather cuffs and the black ink of a cursed tattoo and experienced an odd moment where I didn't exactly recognise myself.

"Yes!" The scream came from across the room. It was followed swiftly by a few ragged cheers, and although I looked in the direction it had come from I saw only a group of eager audience members and nothing of the lucky lady herself.

"Come along, pet," Oliver said, a little louder. "Let us go and see what pleasures there are to be found upstairs."

Dante nodded, Oliver took his hand and the two of them vanished into the crowd heading upstairs.

I wished them luck silently and then looked at Gabriel. My own Master for the evening, I tipped my head to one side and quirked an eyebrow.

"This way," Gabriel said, tugging again on the lead and walking deeper into the house.

There were people everywhere, most of them indulging in delightful excess. I saw a man pouring a bottle of wine into another man's mouth as a woman rode his lap.

In one darkened corner there were at least three people on one chaise, limbs tangled and gender impossible to determine.

I must have been slowing down to watch because Gabriel yanked harder on the leash and pulled me against his side. He leaned down, his mouth near my ear. "Do you see anyone you know?"

I closed my eyes, largely from the heat of his breath and my desire to stop the mission and just go to it with him like so many other people in the place were doing. But he'd asked me a question and I had to answer. "No. Uh. No, Sir."

He nipped my earlobe, which did absolutely nothing to quell my state of arousal, and led me into the next room. In here there were wooden frames and horses assembled, and although a few of them stood empty, at least two were in use - a woman bent over a waist height wooden frame, her arms tied to it with rope as another woman whipped her with a riding crop.

One of the taller frames had a handsome older man strapped to it, and two women were teasing him with feathers.

My trousers were far too constricting, but I didn't dare palm myself through them. If our theories were correct and people here knew who I was, I had to be on my best behaviour, let them think that I was Lucifer's docile little pet and not anything more than that. And that meant not touching myself even when I wanted to.

As if he'd read my mind, Gabriel took a space along the wall of observers and pulled me close to him, pressing my back against his front, and letting his hands play over my chest and waist.

"What do you think, puppy?" He murmured. I pressed back against him and whimpered when I felt his hardness prodding into me. I slipped a hand behind to stroke him.

"I think..." I swallowed, my voice was coming out raspier and more breathy than I had intended. "I think there are a lot of people having a great deal of fun here."

Gabriel chuckled and tugged on the leash, pulling my head back towards his. I could feel the vibration of his voice through my back. "Maybe I ought to make a rack like that for you, perhaps? Would you like it?"

I wanted to reply to him, I really did. I wanted to tell him yes please and how about we try one of them out right now? But all that came out was a whimper of need.

"See anyone you know?"

At least that one didn't require words, I shook my head.

Gabriel lingered a minute longer, both of us enjoying the show that the various people were putting on. Finally he pulled my hand off his crotch and turned me around, kissing me thoroughly before we moved into the corridor to find another crowd of people. The air was hot and everywhere I looked there were people in various stages of undress, enjoying themselves. The smells of sweat and sex were complemented by the scent of melted wax. My heart was thumping and I knew I wouldn't be able to recognise anyone soon enough, not unless I got an orgasm out of the way and I could think straight again.

"Please," I said, my voice reedy with need, pressing myself against his side. "I just need a little please...It's too distracting otherwise."

"You might be right," Gabriel said, surprising me. "There's a lot of... it's very close in here."

His voice was gruff, that same deep roughness it got when he was about to shove his dick inside me. I breathed a sigh of relief.

He pulled me into a room where elegant, sylph-like figures swung on trapezes overhead. Below there was a low table, and people were eating. Well, some of them were eating, some were smearing honey over their lover's skin and licking it off.

Was this what these parties were always like? I should have come to them sober more often. There's so much to see...

Although the sights were beautiful and arousing, I was also feeling close to overwhelmed. Apparently Gabriel was feeling the same way, as all of a sudden he shoved me against the wall and claimed my mouth. He dropped the leash and fiddled with the cuff on my right wrist instead. He yanked my hands together and fastened the cuffs with a silver clip thing I didn't even know he had with him.

Then he pushed my arms up over my head and my trousers down and off, wasting no time in shoving inside me. I thanked my forethought in preparing myself, as I had always used to do before a party where I hoped to meet a new partner.

I wrapped my legs around him and cried out, not at all concerned about the amount of noise I made. It would hardly be heard over all the moaning and crying out others were doing in this room and the next.

Gabriel kept it short and rough, pounding me against the wall until I was sure I'd have bruises from where I kept slamming against it.

His hand stroked me until we both came. My arms had come down to sling around his neck and I was clinging to him, panting hard and aware of the sweat trailing down my back. Gabriel's forehead was pressed against mine, and his hand pumped me twice more before he carefully set me back down, unclipped the cuffs and helped me get my trousers back on.

The whole affair was over in a matter of minutes, but I did feel a lot less distracted, even as I watched Gabriel readjust his clothing.

The release had been needed.

"Right, probably... shouldn't have done that," Gabriel mumbled as he picked up my leash again. "Got a little distracted."

I shook my head and went on tip toes to reply in a hushed voice. "No, it's good, we've blended in," I said. "It's weirder if we were only looking and not... partaking, at all."

"Perhaps you're right," he said. He straightened up, turned and tugged on my leash. "Come on, we'll have to go deeper into the house, I think."

CHAPTER 29

*W*e went further into the depths of the house and the party. I was truly astounded by the number of people present. I began, in fact, to wonder if the local constabulary might be summoned to quiet the party down. Although, as I recalled the Manor wasn't exactly close to its nearest neighbours. I remembered, too, that Dante's friends should be somewhere in the building and wondered if I'd notice them or recognise them as vampires.

We saw debauched sight after debauched sight until it all started to feel a little mundane, but then finally a felt a flash of recognition and grabbed at Gabriel's coat to slow him down.

"Master, wait," I hissed.

He stopped instantly and turned, drawing me closer to him and slipping his hand down to squeeze my arse, no doubt for the benefit of anyone who may be watching although I also appreciated it.

"What is it?" Even though it was loud in the room we were in, he lowered his voice and his cerulean blue eyes flicked back and forth to see who was observing.

"I saw him, the tailor," I said. I looked towards where he'd been a moment before, at a table laden with glasses of champagne, and indeed he was still there, downing a glass as if to steel himself for some task. "Drinking."

Gabriel's gaze followed mine and his grip on me tightened somewhat.

"Keep your eyes on him," he ordered. "Wait here for me. I'll find Dante and Oliver, and we can regroup."

I swallowed, unused to Gabriel trusting me with something like this in the heat of battle. Well, it was hardly a battle was it? And like Gabriel said all I had to do was watch him and not lose him in the crowd.

"Of course," I said. "But hurry back, won't you? I don't want anyone else grabbing at my leash."

Gabriel made a low rumbling sound and unclipped the leash from my collar, pocketing it, and therefore solving the problem.

"Wait, wouldn't it be better if I went, and you watched him?" I asked, a thrill of fear going through me. "What if he recognises me? I can find the others and bring them back."

Gabriel shook his head. "I won't risk losing you in this maze of a house, and besides, I'm taller, I can spot them quicker."

I twisted my mouth to the side, but he did have a point. At least this way he knew where I was..." Give me your coat so I can hide the tattoo then," I hissed.

With a bare second of hesitation, he shrugged off his black frock coat and draped it over my shoulders. I pulled it close across my chest.

"I'll be back as soon as I can." He slipped away, back into the corridor and I spared him a glance, part of me already missing him, wishing he would stay beside me, a tall, powerful, comforting protector.

But he had trusted me with this task, and that was an improvement for sure, so I had to prove myself.

Glancing about, I found myself a recess in the wall with a Greek statue of a young man in it.

"Excuse me," I said to him, and slid in beside him. It was shadowed in there, so I thought I wouldn't be too obvious, and I could see right through to where Victor Phillips, tailor and secret sex cultist was playing with the stem of his wine glass.

He was dressed impeccably, as I would expect. His trousers perfectly tailored in black silk, his waistcoat cut to nip in at his slim waist and accentuate the shape of his chest. It wasn't exactly the provocative or sexual mode of dress most of the other attendees had adopted, but perhaps it was appropriate for the co-host of such an event.

His eyes scanned the room and I shrank back a little towards my marble friend, but his gaze flicked past without any apparent recognition.

Then he did something curious. He tipped his head to one side, as if he were listening. I listened too, but there didn't seem to be anything in particular to listen to. The same moans, groans and flesh on flesh sounds as before.

My eye was caught by a fluttering and I looked up to see a small bird land on the frame of a window. *That's his familiar.*

Victor's eyes narrowed and he frowned, setting his empty glass down on the edge of the table, curiously, right on the edge, with half the base of it over empty air, as if he didn't care if it smashed, or perhaps, wanted to leave it so that it was likely to smash.

He crossed towards the door to the hallway, his strides even and confident, even as he weaved between entwined lovers.

For a moment I was frozen, remembering Gabriel's orders and how they now contradicted themselves. *Keep your eyes on him. Wait here.*

But surely the more important thing was to follow Victor and find out what it was he was up to. The others could find me, Dante could probably sniff me out like a bloodhound, and then we'd all be in the right place where Mister Phillips is.

Far better than waiting here watching nothing, like a dolt.

144

I swallowed, bade goodnight to the marble sculpture and slipped out of the room. Phillips was halfway down the corridor so I hastened my steps and stuck close enough that I could monitor him. I was terrified of his turning and seeing me, for surely he would recognise me just as I had him, but he never looked back.

He was utterly driven, apparently. Making his way deftly through the groups of people lining the halls. He took a stairway up to the next floor, using the grand stairway that led up from the main entrance. There was a large open space there on the landing, with a stone fountain. The fountain appeared to be filled with red wine, not water, and many people were gathered around it, filling glasses or cupping their hands in it and drinking. They were all laughing in the same sort of way, tinkling and delighted. A shiver went up my spine. Although I loved wine dearly, no part of me wanted to go any closer to that fountain.

I shook my head and looked for Philips again, and I saw him replacing the velvet rope that cordoned off a door. Obviously a part of the house that the host didn't want involved in the revelries. Philips looked around, and for a moment I froze, sure he had looked right at me, but his expression didn't so much as flicker, he seemed to look through me as he turned his head back to the door. He let himself in and closed the door behind him.

It was the matter of a second to duck under the rope and ease the door open. My heart thumped, half of me expecting that he would be waiting on the other side to pounce on me. I edged the door open as slowly as I could manage, trying to attract no attention at all. It appeared to work, as I pressed my face to the six inch gap I had made to look inside, there was no eye looking back at me, or hands grabbing at me.

The dimly lit room seemed to be a bedroom. There was a small bed to one side, a wardrobe against the back wall and a large oval mirror. The mirror seemed to be what Philips was interested in, as he walked towards it, apparently entranced by his own reflection. The bird alighted on his shoulder but he didn't pay it any attention.

The mirror was angled slightly towards the door, I could see the reflection of Philips but only darkness behind him. I hoped that he couldn't see me watching, but perhaps that wasn't what I should have worried about. He moved as if he were in a trance, his eyes never wavering from the mirror. It was hard to hear, what with the laughing and splashing from the fountain, but I could see his lips moving.

Then my breath caught and I gripped the door harder, digging my nails in. There was something else in the mirror. It was no longer Philip's reflection, but another figure entirely. Something that didn't move at the same time as him. It was taller, and slimmer. The face was long and alien, with a perfectly straight nose and eyes set far apart, more like a rabbit than a human. It had a copious amount of gloriously thick wavy hair and it was emitting a light that wasn't of this world. The light was pink as the inside of a conch shell, with a tinge of pastel orange. It came flowing, sparkling out of the mirror to warm the room.

My heart pounded in my ears as I watched Philips talk to this thing, which was responding as well. I forced myself to take a breath.

What was that thing? I'd never heard of a mirror thing before.

I wondered for a moment if it was Nab, but he'd never appeared to me in a mirror, and he didn't glow like that. Plus the thing in the mirror, it had a far more feminine energy to it than Nab did. I wasn't sure how I knew that beyond a gut feel, but the more I tried to compare it to Nab the less familiar it felt. I was confident it was something else.

Could this be another descendent of Azathoth the way Naberus was? Or was this something entirely new?

The thing in the mirror laughed and it was simultaneously the most beguiling sound I'd ever heard and utterly discordant. I shuddered, my skin going cold with fright.

I eased myself back from the door and slowly closed it, pressing my back to it and blinking in the more normal lamplight to try and get my heart beat under control.

To my great relief, I saw Gabriel, Dante and Oliver climbing the stairs, Dante in the lead. I ducked back under the velvet rope and threw myself into Dante's arms, letting the fear of the unknown thing drive my actions.

"He's in there," I murmured, against Dante's chest. "And he's talking to a thing in the mirror."

"What was that?" Gabriel's hand found the small of my back and he leaned in, as if kissing Dante.

"Something in the mirror," Dante said, a tone of disbelief to his voice.

Before I could explain myself further, there was a huge crash from somewhere nearby and the floor rumbled under my feet. Dante's arms held me steady to him, but around me the cries of happiness and laughter were replaced with confusion.

I felt a thrill shudder up my spine that made my tattoo prickle. *Someone is here.*

CHAPTER 30

G abriel rushed to the bannister to look down at the floor below, Oliver and Dante each took one of my arms and escorted me over to join him.

The front door to the Manor had been blasted off its hinges, and standing impressively in the doorframe was Natalia Harrow.

She was dressed like some sort of magician. Her dress flowed to the floor but was made of wide lace, exposing her legs below and flashes of skin. She had a long robe of crimson silk over the top, thrown back off her shoulders to display a heavy looking amulet on her chest. Behind her I thought I saw the tall frame of Nab and a few other figures, her lackeys no doubt.

Dante drew me behind him with one arm, but I peeked around, curious.

"It is I!" Natalia shouted, her voice booming curiously through the now largely silent building. "Elder of the Unknowable Way, here to punish the miscreant who splintered from my marvelous and wise guidance!"

Behind me a door slammed open and Philips emerged. I turned, pressing my back to Dante's as he stalked out, the pink and orange glow from the mirror appeared to have attached itself to him somehow, the edges of his face and hands looked almost blurred as he moved, as if the glow was inside him, or emanating out of him. The bird flew behind him and seemed to have grown to the size of a magpie.

Philips' eyes landed on mine and he grinned, his mouth stretching wider than looked comfortable.

"I knew you would come to me, Cedric," he said. "The attraction was too great for you to resist."

Oliver stepped in front of me immediately, he'd picked up a wrought iron candlestick from somewhere and was hefting it in his hand, ready to swing.

"You're not going to lay a finger on him," Oliver said.

"I'm not *that* predictable," I mumbled, stung. I raised my voice a little. "It was Gabriel's plan."

Below us Natalia spoke again, her voice magically enhanced to echo loud. "Come down Victor Philips, and face your punishment!"

A few people gave ragged and confused cheers at this proclamation. It was perhaps, more what they expected from a party such as this one.

Victor's face hardened, and he stalked to the top of the stairs. "Natalia, under your leadership the order has flailed and failed," he said, quite calmly and without raising his voice. But somehow the words carried perfectly. "It is time for a new order, and I have found the source of a true power. One far greater than yours."

Natalia scoffed and advanced into the house, a group of five black robed cultists close behind her. None of them tall enough to be Nab, perhaps I had imagined his form there?

"You wish to challenge me? You're even more of a fool than I thought, Victor! You have no chance against one as powerful as me! I have read the Necromonicon and understood its words. You're nothing but a foolish tailor!"

Several people emerged from the rooms near us and went to

stand behind Phillips, some of them hurriedly pulling on robes of a deep plum. His faction, I supposed.

She stood in the centre of the grand foyer. Party goers all seemed to know to shrink back from her. Philips stood at the top of the stars, glaring down at her. His hands, which had already been glowing, now became incandescent with pinkish light and I felt the thrum of magic in the air. Oppressive, like the pressure in your ears when you descended from height. The hairs on my arms all stood to attention and Oliver took a step back, pressing me back against Dante again.

"You have come here tonight to do what? Overcome me? Steal the boy from within these walls? You shall not!"

Phillips raised a hand, glowing now so strongly it hurt the eye to look at it, and pointed at Natalia Harrow. The light shot out of his hand and would have struck her, except that she spoke a word and a sheet of weird smoke coalesced in front of her, forming a shield. My back prickled again, my tattoo seemed to be responding to the magic Harrow was doing, and I felt a thrum of something urgent shoot down my arm and to my fingertips.

Oliver had shoved me behind him again, and I stumbled over Dante's ankle and grabbed the bannister to steady myself so I didn't fall. That was good, gripping the cool wood distracted me from the weird sensation of magic inside me. I flexed my hands and gripped the bannister, not wanting to let the magic spill out.

This movement, and probably Phillips' words, alerted Harrow to my presence and she cackled with a horrible, cruel glee.

"Cedric! My dear boy, your time has come at last!"

I hauled myself properly upright to glare down at her. I had been afraid a moment before, but her words banished my fear and set me alight with anger instead.

"Fuck you, Harrow," I shouted, my voice projecting louder

and deeper than I had expected. "And fuck the cult, you can all go jump in the sea as far as I care!"

I glanced back at Phillips, in case he was going to intervene and saw that Gabriel, Dante and Oliver had formed a protective circle around me. Backs to me, weapons drawn. Well, Oliver had a candlestick, Dante had a knife and Gabriel a modestly sized cutlass.

"He's mine," Phillips said, apparently ignoring what I'd said about the cult. "And you shall not prevail!"

Natalia had been doing something with her hands as this happened and I felt a ripple in the air of magic again. The sort of magic that came from beyond the stars, rather than beyond the mirror.

"They're really going to do it," I said, softly but loud enough that my lovers could hear. "They're going to fight with magic."

Natalia let her magic go and it manifested in a dozen small flying things, dark matter made into something birdlike, but infinitely stranger, as they had no heads or faces, just oddly pointed wings and long forked tails in the back.

Dante hissed. "They'll bring down the building and everyone in it."

"We have to protect the innocent people," Oliver said. Although it did occur to me that due to the nature of the party, innocent was a relative term, but my heart had swelled so much with the pure wholesomeness of his statement that I couldn't do it.

Phillips cried out as the black flying things descended on him. For a moment his head was clouded with the things, then he shouted and they all spun away, stunned. His bird grew larger, or perhaps the glowing light around it just made it look bigger.

I watched in horror as two of the black flying things redirected their attack to some of the people clustered around the red wine fountain, and the rest dove on Phillips again.

He stretched his hands out and a clear crystal sword manifested in them, which he used to swipe at the things. My tattoo flamed with heat and I felt the unholy sensation of it moving on my skin again. The pain was less excruciating than before, but still present. I groaned as softly as I could.

The people who had pulled on purple robes to support Phillips ran past him, trying to get to Harrow and tripping on the stairs. Her black robed followers rushed up to meet them, and from lower in the house some more appeared. Had they been lying in wait for her to arrive?

Gabriel glanced at me and exhaled loudly. "Oliver is right. Dante, you stay with Cedric, protect him. Cedric, try and get out without being grabbed by a cultist. Oliver and I will ensure no more lives are lost than necessary."

"Yes, Captain," Dante said.

Oliver whirled towards me, kissed me on the mouth, winked once and then dashed off, swinging the candlestick at the black things Harrow had created or summoned.

Gabriel didn't kiss me, but he did shoot me a look that seemed full of something... longing perhaps, or a desire to say something he couldn't. I shook my head, and he ran to follow Oliver.

I looked down to see Harrow had advanced towards the staircase. Phillips, who had now defeated the swarm, was striding towards me with an intent look. The bird behind him had incorporated some of the weird purple light into itself and seemed to be making large wings behind his back.

I didn't want to fight him, I didn't want to let this power take control of me again. I didn't want to let the power loose and hurt anyone again.

But the power. I can feel it. It surges inside me and I can feel it. It's lighting up my veins and it won't be denied.

"I'll protect you," Dante said. I wanted to take his hand, but I remembered all too clearly what had happened to Dante the last time I had let the power in my tattoo loose.

"Thank you Dante, but it might be safer if you get behind me," I said. With Harrow on the stairs and Phillips closing in, it didn't seem like a smart idea to run and hide. Which left surrendering or fighting as my options, and I found that my blood was singing in my veins and demanding a fight. There was no choice now.

The pain in my back intensified and I felt the power shoot down my arms, ready to use. I gritted my teeth and lifted my chin.

Phillips raised his hand and the sparkling pink light intensified.

Time to show them what I'm really capable of.

CHAPTER 31

IN WHICH SOME INNOCENT PERVERTS ARE RESCUED

Once he had the order from Captain Gabriel, Oliver wasted no time. He bade Cedric a quick farewell, smiling and winking despite the butterfly of dread in his chest, and sprinted to the nearby fountain where several people in various states of disarray were battling against the weird magical flying things Natalia Harrow had summoned.

He swung the candlestick he'd picked up and it passed right through one of the things, which seemed to dissolve it. It dissipated into black dust.

"Brilliant," Oliver said.

Gabriel destroyed the other one with his sword and the two of them helped the revellers up. "There are back stairs," Gabriel said. "The servant's access, through that door." He pointed the way with his sword and, wide-eyed, the revellers hurried that way,

Oliver saw people clustered in the doorway of a nearby room, watching the dramatic magic battle with a mixture of confusion and fear. He shouted to them, directing them to the door the others had used. "Get out, it's not safe!"

Gabriel took a more direct approach, perhaps something in his years of leading a pirate crew had taught him that sometimes people needed action rather than words. He strode to the room and yanked one of the observers out by the arm. "That way, go down the servant's stairs and get to your carriage!"

That seemed to break the reverie that the group had been caught in, and they did as he ordered with only a minimum of fuss.

Behind Gabriel and Oliver, Cedric had joined the battle with the magic he possessed. Oliver hesitated, watching aghast as the initial energy blast from his hands hit Phillips like a slap across the face. He stopped walking, stumbling to a stop, and his head snapped hard to one side.

He retaliated with a swirling, mist-like sheet of light that stretched from the ceiling to the floor, advancing towards Cedric to snare him like a net.

Cedric's next blast of power punched a hole through it, then Harrow got to the top of the stairs and sent another swarm of flying black things to confound the both of them. Oliver found he was distracted, watching the weird display.

The last people had left the room and he swallowed, forcing himself to look away and track where Gabriel had gone. There, he was in another room across the landing. Oliver sprinted to join him, deliberately banishing any worries for Cedric or Dante from his mind. He had a job to do, and he would do it.

From Dante's perspective, everything was escalating far too fast. The way Cedric's eyes blazed with a cold, white light that Dante recognised from the night sky and not anything living chilled his heart. Then he was distracted by the way the tiles cracked underfoot when Phillips's eldritch light dissipated onto it, and always his hackles were up from the piercing *wrongness* of the things Harrow was summoning.

This wrongness was compounded by the sheer weirdness of the magic Phillips was harnessing. The eldritch light wasn't anything Dante had seen before, and something about it gave him a bad taste, in a magical sense. The discordance of both these magics raised his defenses up as high as they could go and heightened his need to get out and get Cedric out with him.

He knew from experience there were seldom true winners from a magical fight such as this. It was all ego and an addiction to the power that magic gave.

He had some small power of his own, blood magic that could be harnessed with ritual and with bleeding, but it was precious little help now.

The best chance he had to protect the innocents in the building, and to save Cedric, was to get through whatever power currently had a hold on him with and appeal to his emotions and with logic.

"Cedric!" he was close enough to Cedric still that he didn't have to shout, but he raised his voice a little all the same. "Sunshine, listen to me."

Cedric's head twitched, as if he were trying to turn to Dante and then changed his mind, or perhaps, was stopped.

Harrow's latest summoned beasts took the form of long legged dogs or wolves. Thin and far too pointed to be at all natural, with long snouts and no eyes. They raced from the folds of her robe as if it were a portal to another world.

Perhaps it is, Dante thought. The idea disquieted him on a cellular level, but he had to maintain his focus. Simply speaking didn't appear to be getting through to Cedric entirely, so he had to do something more.

Although loathe to introduce more magic to the already chaotic scene, Dante saw he had little choice. Blood magic requires blood, so he sliced into his own forearm with his knife.

The iron smell hit his nose instantly and he felt his fangs pop and his senses sharpen. He had to pick his moment, however. There was no sense in distracting Cedric at the moment he was under attack. Cedric sent another blast of power, a much larger one this time, which rebounded off Harrow's defences and struck the balustrade, shattering it and raining pieces of wood down into the lobby. Dante's ears picked up the sound of human screams and his nose the smell of blood, not his this time. The vampire part of him became ferociously hungry and tried to pull him towards those already hurt and weak. He could feed so well, so abundantly and none would be the wiser...

Dante dismissed the base instincts he had spent centuries acclimating to, and focused again on the fight.

Now was his moment.

Harrow's hounds were racing towards Phillips, and Phillips had his full attention on another net, looking to ensnare the hounds.

Dante put a hand on Cedric's shoulder and used the vampiric power of compulsion to put urgency into his words.

"Cedric stop it, follow me to safety." He put every ounce of willpower into the words and it did work, Cedric lowered his hands and turned to look at him.

"Dante?" He said, confused as if waking from a deep sleep.

"Yes, Cedric, focus on me and let's go."

He started walking backwards, trying to draw Cedric with him by tugging on his arm and for a handful of steps it worked. But a ground shaking crash distracted Cedric enough to stop him walking.

Dante looked towards the sound and saw that the grand chandelier that hung in the foyer had been brought down by more of Harrow's summoned flying things. With horror, he saw that there were more and more *things* spilling out of her cloak and into the Manor. From her expression she wasn't entirely in control of this, but her attention was mostly on the tailor, Philips, who had somehow grown taller. Huge wings flapping behind him.

No, he hasn't grown, it's a glamour, Dante thought. The odd taste of Phillips's magic then made sense to Dante. There was a fae element to it, something that had leaked through from a different world. But it was clearly distinct from the power Harrow was harnessing.

If Phillips had made a deal with the fae then there was even more at stake than first appeared. No one had seen any fae for generations, but Dante could remember further back than that.

He looked around for something made of iron. *The candlestick that Oliver had picked up, did it have a twin?*

Distracted, he went in search of another piece of iron.

It was then that Cedric's powers amplified again, spurred on perhaps by the magical boasting that Phillips and Harrow were doing.

Harrow was swirling her cloak from side to side, creatures of shadow and something even darker than shadow, the darkness of the space between the stars were pouring out into the Manor. Some flew, some stalked on overly long legs and some skittered across the floor like large spidery crabs. She was shouting and crowing. "The boy is mine! The ritual has been twice attempted, and thrice will be the success! You cannot imagine that your interference will slow my ambition!"

The tailor had grown to nine or ten feet tall and his fingers had elongated. His nose and jaw as well, giving him a birdlike demeanor. His magic spread from his fingers like spiderwebs, sticking to the walls and floor as he advanced towards Cedric, intent on claiming him.

"He has escaped you twice, more than that! He has evaded you at every turn! It is time for a new Master! A new leader for those who would learn the truth, and I am that Master! Cedric my boy, you always liked the way I dressed you. Let me do so again..."

Cedric, his head whipping swiftly back and forth, trying to keep his eyes on both of the magicians, let the power of the tattoo, the power of the eldritch god from beyond the stars, flow through him once more.

Dante looked up in time to see the tentacled tattoo on his back writhe and then, horribly, to lift its inky arms off his skin to wave in the air behind his head.

Cedric spoke a word, "Azathoth", and power exploded from him. The blast was indiscriminate, not directed with any care or in any particular direction. The tiles at Cedric's feet cracked apart, sending shards of ceramic flying. Harrow, Phillips and the few cultists who were grappling with each other at the top of the stairs were thrown off their feet, and one in a black robe went over the balustrade and crashed to the ground below.

The force of it had an effect on Cedric himself, and he swayed, his arms by his sides, his tattoo swirling bodily around him like a visible wind.

"Cedric!" Dante cried and ran to him. He swept Cedric into his arms, heedless of the possible danger of the cursed tattoo, and used the moment that both magicians were picking themselves back up to flee down the servant's stairs.

Dante's vampiric speed had them out the door in moments, and he perhaps would have continued to run all the way back to the ship, except he saw Gabriel slumped over a fence, face first, his limbs limp.

Dante skidded to a stop and approached the captain. "Captain? Gabriel, are you all right?"

Gabriel lifted his head and groaned. "Yes, I'll live, I think, Oliver... he went in for the last of the ..." His voice broke off into a rasping, rattling cough.

Dante looked back at the house. The windows had blown out over half the building, and there were alternate flashes of blue, green, pink and purple lights, telling him the battle between Harrow and Phillips was continuing.

He started to lower Cedric to the ground, to prop him against the fence with the Captain, when Oliver came out.

Dante, who hadn't wanted to let go of his young lover anyway, straightened up and readjusted his hold on him.

He had put his jacket around the shoulders of a young woman who didn't seem to have anything else on, and his shirt was hanging open on a young man. Both of them looked terrified, in shock most likely. Once in the night air they thanked Oliver and bolted towards where the carriages were parked.

"That's the last two. Oh, thank the stars you got Cedric out." Oliver had a bag slung over his shoulder, he seemed winded but otherwise unhurt.

"He's not in a good way, but the captain has it worse I think," Dante said. "I can manage both of them, if you help with the Captain."

Oliver looked set to protest, even reached a hand out towards Cedric, but retracted it again as the tattoo moved. Dante sensed from proximity that the power Cedric had called upon was easing off him but it was still present. He hauled him onto one shoulder and held out his other arm as Oliver helped Gabriel up. Together, they limped awkwardly back to the ship.

CHAPTER 32

IN WHICH THE WOUNDED ARE TENDED TO

I woke up with a thumping pain in my head and muscle aches all over. I felt as if I had been beaten all over with sticks and then run the length of London. I groaned and buried my head in the pillow it was resting on, trying to go back to sleep so I could escape the pain.

The falling asleep plan wasn't going well. The thumping in my head seemed to intensify the more I tried to drift off and eventually I flopped over onto my back and huffed, starting at the ceiling. Whatever I'd been drinking the night before had really done a number on me.

What had I been doing last night, anyway? I knew I was in Kingston, of course I was in Kingston, that was where I lived... wasn't it?

No, that wasn't right. The ship, and Dante...

It was light out, I could see that, but it was the grey early morning light of just past dawn, not mid morning. I was on the ship, I could tell we were moving as well. The swell of the waves beneath us. And last night we'd been at the... yes, the Hellfire club party.

The events of the night before, and indeed, the last eight or so months came back to me slowly, dripping honey-like through my memory and into my awareness with somewhat alarming slowness.

Finally I recalled that something inside me had... well, it had taken control, hadn't it? It had me say that awful thing's name and then power like I'd never felt before had flooded my body and come out like a tidal wave. The details of the fight were blurry, and I couldn't at all remember how it had ended. There was only blackness, a loss of consciousness, perhaps, which explained why I felt like I had a hangover now.

I was in Oliver's cabin, I thought, as I looked around. That was strange. I managed myself into a half sitting position propped on the pillows and groaned when my head swam. I felt weak as a kitten.

There was a wine bottle full of water beside the bed so I uncorked it and had a long drink. I could feel the coolness of it all the way down my throat and into my chest.

The door opened and Marco came in. He looked relieved to see me sitting up. "Cedric, you're awake, that's wonderful. How are you feeling?"

I swallowed, already wanting more water. "Like the worst hangover I've ever had."

He looked cautiously concerned. "Do you want a bucket?"

I took a moment to consider this question because usually my hangovers did involve some emptying of the stomach, but that part of me felt fine. "No, just... more water," I said, and sated my own need with another swig of the bottle. I took a deep breath and sat all the way up. "How did the others fare?"

"The Captain's in a pretty bad way," Marco said. "Perhaps you could come and see him, if you're up for it?"

That sent ice water through my veins and I was up in a moment. I pulled on a clean shirt of Oliver's that was draped on a wooden chair, then some folded linen trousers, left out for me.

My heart was in my mouth as I tried to recall the last time I'd seen Gabriel. He'd been right there beside me, and then I wasn't sure.

I followed Marco through the ship to the Captain's cabin, my mind full of horrible thoughts and fears. Fears that I'd have to say goodbye to him, that this was the last time he'd say my name or call me 'puppy', that he was going to die.

In the cabin, Gabriel was sprawled on the bed, his eyes closed and his face an unusually pale colour. His shirt was off, and there was a bandage wound tightly around his chest and shoulder.

Oliver was winding fresh bandages beside the bed, his expression serious. He looked up at me, his eyes meeting mine for a moment before looking at my shoulder and then my neck as well. "Morning, Cedric, are you all right?"

"I'm all right, just feel wrung out. What happened?" I asked. I was at a loss for what to do. I wanted to sit on the bed beside Gabriel and take his hand but I didn't want to jostle his wound or wake him up. I wanted to help Oliver but I didn't want to get in the way of what he was doing. I wanted... I wanted Gabriel to not be hurt.

"We were down on the ground floor, in the lobby, after Natalia Harrow had gone to the stairs," Oliver said. He set down the bandage he'd been folding and swallowed. "We were getting some people out the back way, through the kitchen. You know some of those rich assholes had left their partners tied up and just ran for it?" Oliver's voice trembled with anger, and I felt a similar wave of outrage myself, but he was being careful to speak in low tones and not wake Gabriel.

"That's abhorrent."

"It is. Anyway, we were getting the trapeze artists out when there was a big loud sound from upstairs and some of the balustrade shattered, I guess. It came right down on us. Gabriel shoved me and a girl out of the way and took the worst of it."

For the second time that morning ice water flooded my

veins. I remembered something about the balustrade, didn't I? Had that been my blast that shattered it?

I couldn't remember clearly but suddenly my stomach didn't seem as settled as I'd thought it was.

"It pierced his chest and there are some splintered bits in his shoulder, I've done my best to get them all out, I think I have. But he lost a lot of blood, kept going for a few minutes after the thing hit him, I have no idea how. Perhaps the adrenaline kept him..." Oliver shook his head. "But I think he'll live as long as we can keep infection out."

I didn't like how unsure Oliver sounded. My stomach turned over and I swallowed down some bile that had risen in my throat. "Then we'll work hard and keep the infection out, right?"

"Right."

I tore my eyes from Gabriel's pallid face and properly looked at Oliver. He hadn't slept, had he? That's what he'd said, he'd been operating on Gabriel... He'd done so much to help people at the party, he'd rescued so many, and then he'd rescued the Captain as well. While I was... what? Possessed by a monster? A monster that had done... *I don't want to finish that thought. But there is something I can do right now to help.*

"Go and get some sleep, Ollie," I said, my voice breaking a little. "You really need it, and some food and water."

Oliver looked at Gabriel and his expression wavered, but the bags under his eyes seemed to stand out even more.

"I mean it. I'll stay with him, and if anything changes, I'll let you know."

He looked back at me, and must have seen the resolve in my eyes. I hoped that's what he'd seen, and not the fear or the squashed down guilt that it could have been... *no.*

"All right," he said, finally. I went to give him a hug and kissed his cheek. It wasn't my imagination that he seemed to stiffen just at first when I touched him, but he relaxed almost instantly. I put it aside. "If the bandage goes red, if you see it seeping blood, change it, and clean it," he pointed at a stout bottle of clear alcohol. "Or come and get me and I'll do it. If he wakes up see if you can get him to drink something."

I nodded. "I'll do my best."

Oliver left, and I brought the chair to the side of the bed, sat down and watched Gabriel's chest rise and fall. It felt like this was the most important task I'd ever been given, to just watch. And the idea occurred to me that if I didn't keep watching, maybe it would stop moving and then he'd be gone.

And it would be my fault, wouldn't it?

Can't I remember letting the power come out of me in a blast that broke things? Broke a section of balustrade off and sent it falling into the foyer?

Can't I hear it crashing in my memory?

Was it even me that did that or was it... the thing inside me?

I'm a monster.

CHAPTER 33

IN WHICH SOME THINGS FESTER AND SOME BEGIN TO HEAL

I don't know how long I sat like that, watching Gabriel's chest rise and fall, and hating myself. It did, once more, occur to me that perhaps it would be better for all the people I cared about if I just left the ship. Left the ship and well, not turned myself into the cultists, because then they'd just kill me and open up the portal to another world.

But maybe I could lose myself somewhere they'd never find me.

In some ways it was a noble thought, but I also knew that I'd never do it.

The idea of a place where no one knew me, and I tried to keep it that way? Not knowing anyone, getting no attention and no affection? I wouldn't last a week.

It wasn't an option. And besides, Oliver would worry. No, we had to do more to remove the curse. The whole point of infiltrating the party was to find out more, to learn who these people were and how they'd cast the spell.

Instead I'd got distracted and had sex with Gabriel and then done my best to kill him, apparently.

Granted, Harrow gate crashing had rather put a dampener

on our plans. We hadn't expected that, and it had vastly cut into the time we'd had to investigate.

Maybe if I hadn't been so driven by my unquenchable need for sex this wouldn't have happened. We could have learned more...

My thoughts spiralled, always coming back to the same points. This was my fault and I had no idea how to absolve myself. How to get rid of the curse and protect my friends.

The door opened and I startled, half in a daze, half hypnotised by the steady rise and fall of Gabriel's chest.

"Cedric, how are you?" Dante was at my side in an instant, his hand in mine and his eyes searching my face.

I nodded. "I mean, all right. I feel weak, I suppose, worn out, but I'm all right." My gaze slid back to Gabriel.

"Good, how much do you remember?" Dante asked.

I shook my head. "Not enough, I have no idea what I did beyond..."

Dante squeezed my hand and kissed my cheek. "What happened, it wasn't your fault. The curse, it took hold of you, I think."

A spark of hope that had flared when he said it wasn't my fault was instantly extinguished. The curse had taken hold, my curse. It *was* my fault.

"Oh."

Dante turned to look at Gabriel. "How's he doing?"

I shook my head. "Fine, I think. The bandage hasn't soaked through, and he's breathing very evenly."

"I offered him some of my blood," Dante said, softly, his voice heavy with sadness. "It would have healed him fully."

I caught my breath. From the way Dante was talking it didn't sound like Gabriel had agreed to this as a course of action.

"He said no?" I said, finally.

"He said not yet," Dante said. He smiled ruefully and turned back to me. "He'll pull through with careful care, and Marco was able to put a small healing spell on him. If we can get to somewhere with a kind witch it'd be even better. But it's his body, he decides what happens to it."

That statement hit me like a punch to the gut and I felt tears well in my eyes. Because it was just now occurring to me that I didn't have that luxury at all. My body wasn't my own any longer, I was sharing it with something else, something malevolent.

Dante saw the change in me and pulled me into his arms, holding me close. But I didn't want to give in and cry. Not right now. I had to be strong right then, and I had to save what I needed to say until all my lovers were present and awake. But I leaned into Dante and smelled his delightful smell of blood and musk and let his strength steel my backbone.

"I've got you, and Gabriel's safe," Dante said. "You're safe."

"I'm not though," I said, fighting an urge to pull back from him, suddenly incensed. "I'm like a lit fuse, aren't I?"

Dante shook his head. "No, you're a boy. A young man, and you're my sunshine."

I wished it was that simple, I really did. So for that moment I closed my eyes and tried to believe it.

The next day Gabriel was sitting up on his own and eating a little broth. He would fall asleep every twenty minutes or so, and he was clearly in a lot of pain, but he didn't complain. Just tried to micromanage Dante's running of the ship. Our destination was Tortuga, I found out, because it had largely been a safe harbour and a familiar place for Gabriel to recuperate.

I spent some more time in Gabriel's cabin, but I slept in Dante's room with him. Oliver was trying to hide it, but he was still acting skittish around me. He would meet my eyes but only briefly, and I felt like I was making him uncomfortable.

When I was in Gabriel's cabin, watching Oliver change his bandage, or administer a herbal concoction for the pain, I felt irritated. I couldn't place my finger on it for hours after I'd stalked out. To busy myself I had thought to paint, or sketch, but when I looked at my supplies my stomach turned. I couldn't risk any kind of event where the curse intervened again.

Instead I ended up in the galley with the cook, peeling potatoes and doing the small, boring tasks that needed doing. This gave me more time with my thoughts, as the cook was a quiet man. They spiralled on the curse again, and how it was my fault the captain was hurt, and how if he died it would be on my hands...

And then I thought on why it should irritate me to see Oliver taking such good care of Gabriel, and finally I realised the sad truth of it.

I was jealous.

Not jealous that Gabriel was getting the attention, not at all. Jealous of how gentle Oliver was being. How there was a tenderness there, a mutual respect I felt separated from.

Did I feel like Gabriel and Oliver didn't respect me? Or was this all tied in again with my thought that the only thing I had to offer any of them was my body?

I mulled it all over and peeled potatoes and generally felt morose until there wasn't anything left to do in the kitchen but get out of the way.

I went back up onto deck in time to see Dante handing the helm over to Bilal.

"Cedric, there you are. Oliver has said we should talk about what happened last night, in Gabe's cabin."

Gabe? Since when is Dante calling Gabriel Gabe? Is Gabriel calling him Dan in response?

Fighting down another wave of annoyance, I followed him into Gabriel's cabin. Inside, Gabriel was using his left hand to wipe his face with a damp cloth and Oliver was looking over a book at his desk. They made such a handsome pair, didn't they?

Perhaps I was foolish to imagine the four of us could share something all together.

Maybe Dante and I should leave them to it, or perhaps I should leave all three of them...

I shook my head, dismissing that thought. Probably our arrangement couldn't last, but I could try and enjoy it for now.

Oliver looked up, smiled at Dante and me and then snapped the book shut. "Thanks for coming," he said. "I just thought we ought to discuss what happened last night, while it's still fresh."

CHAPTER 34

"Right," I said. "Well, there was a magic battle and my tattoo activated itself."

The others looked at me with various expressions of confusion and fear. "It activated itself?" Oliver said, finally.

"Yes, the power started flowing and I tried to hold it back and then I couldn't, and then I don't remember much of anything." I looked at Gabriel and quickly looked away again, guilt flooding over me.

"You told me to get behind you," Dante said. "You seemed very determined, your mind already made up."

I sighed heavily and shook my head. "I know, I remember that bit, but please, you have to believe me. It was as if I was looking at myself doing it from outside. I could feel myself trying not to do it, and it was hopeless, the power, my tattoo, it was already..." I trailed off. I knew they had no reason to believe me. I had happily used my power so many times even knowing how dangerous it was. "I'm sorry," I said. Feeling defeated, I looked at the boards under my feet. I might as well come totally clean and let them all hate me the way they ought to. "I think it's my fault Gabriel was hurt. I can remember there was a blast and it went wide, hit the balustrade. That was my fault, my power."

For a moment no one said anything, and I let the silence stretch. They needed time to process this, just as I had been trying and failing to.

I startled as an arm went around me. Dante again, loyal, beautiful, trustworthy Dante. "Cedric," he said, softly. "It's not your fault. None of us think that."

I scoffed at that. In response he lifted my chin with his finger and made me look at Gabriel, whose expression was soft. "I don't blame you at all," Gabriel said. "There was a lot happening, and it was my choice to push people out of the way and take the brunt of the blow."

"And we could all see that the curse was affecting you," Oliver said, matter of factly. His matter-of-fact assuredness brought me some comfort. "Your eyes had started to glow sort of, and your tattoo..." the assuredness was gone, and my throat went dry. "Besides you fell unconscious, it's not like you'd have done that to yourself on purpose."

"What about my tattoo?"

I had checked myself in a mirror and the tattoo hadn't got bigger again, thankfully. But it did seem to be slightly more indelible, like the black of the magical ink was blacker, or there were more symbols and swirls on the design.

Oliver looked pleadingly at Dante. "Please tell him?"

"Tell me what?"

Dante squeezed me closer and then let go to move to look me in the eyes. "Your tattoo, it did something none of us have seen before. It was... well, it was like it was a living thing, lifting off your skin."

The aforementioned skin went cold and all my hairs stood up. "It what?"

Dante swallowed. I looked over at Oliver. "You saw this too?"

"You'd passed out by then," he said. "But yes, it was like a mystical effect. The skin on your arms was bare."

I looked at my forearms. With the sleeves of the shirt I wore rolled up, the tentacle tattoos were plainly visible. "You couldn't see these?"

"I could see them, they were..." he raised his arms and waved them back and forth in the air, demonstrating how it must have looked.

"As I said, nothing any of us have seen before," Dante said again. He pulled me against his side, but I resisted, wrapping my arms around my middle.

"I'm so fucked. I can't... maybe I should just... should just..." I didn't know exactly how to finish that sentence. I knew I couldn't leave, I'd been over that a thousand times in the last day.

Oliver hurried over as well. I was standing but he pulled me onto the end of the bed, and tucked me under his arm. Dante went to his knees in front of me, demanding I look him in the eye. "Do you remember what I said yesterday, Cedric?"

I didn't want to say the words out loud, but he wasn't going to let them slide either. "It wasn't my fault. But it is, I'm the one with the curse on me!" *And I'm worthless. I'm going to get them all killed.* "I'm going to get you all killed."

"Cedric, we have a say in what we will and won't do," Oliver said. "I didn't have to follow you to sea, did I? I chose that."

"Well, yes, but I didn't tell you it was a pirate ship."

"Cedric," Gabriel said. His voice wasn't as powerful as usual. *Because of me.* "You're not blaming yourself for getting cursed are you?"

I swallowed. Was I? I was blaming myself for the effect the curse was having. That I had been cursed in the first place? Maybe.

"I don't know," I breathed.

"None of us blame you for being cursed," Gabriel said. "Or for the curse taking over your body. That is some shit beyond your control."

A knot loosened in my chest. Apparently, I'd needed to hear that said.

"I agree," Oliver said. "It's not your fault what the curse does with your body."

The tears I hadn't let myself shed alone with Dante the day before welled up again. "You're all in danger though, just from my being near."

Oliver and Dante both hugged me at once, Dante around my waist and Oliver around my shoulders and I had to choke out a laugh.

"If I wasn't injured I'd take the other side," Gabriel said. He nudged me with his foot. "We want you to be safe, that's why we went to that blasted party in the first place."

I sighed, smiling, leaning against Oliver and feeling something coming unwound inside me. "But we didn't get anything from the party, did we? Did anyone see if Natalia Harrow died?"

Dante shook his head. "We left while the battle was still going. I have to assume one of them is dead though."

"I should..." I realised I'd been holding back something else from them and now seemed like the best time to confess. "I should tell you that my dreams, they've been different. I've been seeing Nab, uh, Naberus. But in real life as well as in dreams. He came to the ship and we talked. He said my powers, that I could use them."

Dante sat back on his heels and frowned. "When?"

"A few times. He warned me of the warlock, of the tailor, I guess. He said it was a rival to Harrow."

"Some truth in what he says and some lies as well," Oliver sighed and rested his head against mine.

"Why didn't you mention this to us earlier?" Gabriel asked.

I swallowed, because truly I wasn't sure why I hadn't. It had been strange, really. I'd meant to, but I hadn't. Then it dawned on me. "I think there was a compulsion not to," I said. "Does that sound likely? Nab made it so I didn't or couldn't tell you. But it's gone now."

"Blasted away by your own powers, perhaps," Dante mused.

"The good news is that I managed to steal some books from the Manor before we got out," Oliver said.

"You did?" Dante and Gabriel didn't seem surprised so I guessed they already knew, or maybe Gabriel had even given the task to Oliver as a secret mission.

"Yes, I don't know how much help they'll be, and I only got a few things, but maybe they will have something useful in there. It will take me some time to go through them of course."

"I should be able to get back to work tomorrow," Gabriel said. "Not having to look after me all the time should give you more opportunity to study."

"You need longer on bed rest than that." Oliver let go of me to give Gabriel a stern look. "Don't even think about leaving that bed until sundown tomorrow at least."

"Speaking of which, we should leave the Captain to rest," Dante said.

CHAPTER 35

IN WHICH CEDRIC AND HIS LOVERS PLEDGE
THEMSELVES TO EACH OTHER

*S*undown the next day was far too optimistic, but two days later Gabriel had begun to rally and his complexion was more or less back to normal. He even got up for a walk around the deck and had a full meal.

Dante, Oliver, and I had taken it in shifts to stay with him during his recuperation and in that time I had come to feel more reassured that their words were not just words. They truly didn't blame me for being cursed, for accidentally hurting Gabriel. They wanted me to be safe and happy.

Oliver had also been spending time decoding the books he'd stolen from the Manor, because apparently they weren't just books you could pick up and read, they were books written in ciphers and codes. It sounded like an absolute nightmare to me, but Oliver was loving the challenge of it, and filling pages with his workings and attempts.

I had continued to sleep in Dante's room, to give Gabriel space and to rest and recover. It was always pleasant to sleep against Dante, for his skin was cool and I found myself less prone to overheating. Also I liked to help him feed, and it was very convenient and pleasant in the morning or late at night when we were laying in bed together for him to bite my wrist or my neck or perhaps my thigh and drink his fill. It brought us closer together still, and made me feel more in my own body, which was a welcome sensation.

Finally, one night, Gabriel invited me back into his bed. The way it happened, Oliver had changed Gabriel's bandages while I was reading in the cabin.

"It's healing nicely," Oliver had said. "How's the pain?"

Gabriel shook his head. "A little itching around where the stitches were perhaps, nothing bothering me."

In fact, most of the stitches had come out the day before and although Oliver had worried over another possible chance of infection, luck seemed to be on our side this time.

"He's hardly napped at all today," I added. "He really does seem better."

"I feel better," Gabriel added. "In fact, I think I'm better enough for some company tonight if you can bear to drag yourself away from Dante, Cedric?"

I grinned, snapping the book shut. "Of course."

"And I should like to show my appreciation for your care," Gabriel said. "If you'd agree to join us, Oliver?"

Oliver flushed with a smile. "I should like that, I think."

"And Dante, too?" I asked, although I was fairly confident of the answer. Gabriel gave me a lascivious wink and I got up out of the chair. "I'll go and get him now."

"Just, hold on, let me secure this bandage," Oliver said. "And we'll have to be a little gentle with the Captain." He fussed with the muslin and I went to fetch Dante.

We were a day or so out from Tortuga, and although there had been some sightings of things in the ocean, more monsters perhaps, they had apparently kept their distance from us. I suspected it was just the crew being superstitious rather than an actual threat.

"Dante," I called out, hardly able to contain the glee in my voice. "Captain wants you in his bed... chamber."

With a laugh, Bilal took the helm and Dante shook his head, tied his hair back in a low ponytail and took my hand. "Glad to hear you're back to your old self, sunshine."

"Me? It's the Captain who's been recuperating."

"I think it's been you, as well," Dante replied. He squeezed my hand, then tugged me back and into his arms. "I take it from your terribly subtle hint that I'm about to walk into a four way?"

"I believe so," I said, snuggling my cheek against his chest, feeling butterflies of happiness in my chest for the first time in many days.

We made our way into Gabriel's cabin and closed the door behind us. Oliver and the captain were already kissing, Oliver kneeling on the bed beside him and Gabriel gently cupping Oliver's cheek. It was a sweeter scene than I had expected to walk into, but one that thrilled me all the same.

"Let me help you with those," Dante murmured. He made quick work of undressing me and setting my shirt and trousers aside, so I returned the favour, making sure to drag my fingertips over every sensitive part of him as it was revealed. Dante responded not by pulling me closer or kissing me, but by turning me around and gently propelling me to the bed.

"Quite right," I said, feeling a little lightheaded with anticipation. "Must get to the main event."

Oliver turned and offered me his hand, which I took, leaning on him a little as I hauled myself up on the bed beside him. Gabriel was laid out before us like a banquet table and I leaned in to kiss him.

"What do we need to be careful of, aside from the obvious?" Dante asked. He'd climbed up at the end of the bed and was positioning himself between Gabriel's legs, licking his lips.

Oliver gently scratched my back with his fingernails as he replied. "Anything that could wrench the shoulder would be bad. It's best if Gabriel stays lying back like this."

Gabriel grumbled and broke the kiss. "Hang on, I wanted to fuck Cedric, and then Dante..."

"You can," I said, quickly. "We'll ride you." A terribly wicked idea came to me then and I caught Oliver's eye. "What if we tied Gabriel down, you know, so he doesn't wrench anything?"

Oliver's face split into a wide grin that was even more wicked than my idea had been. "Well, that is an idea..."

"Hang on..." Gabriel said again. His cheeks were flushed in a way I wasn't sure I'd seen before. *Was he actually going to agree to this? I never thought I'd see the day when dominant Gabriel gave up control.*

"Only with your permission, of course," I said. I leaned in to kiss his neck, giving him some pleasure as he considered.

"We couldn't raise his arms up, they'd have to be down by his sides, but perhaps it would be safest," Oliver said. He trailed his fingers over Gabriel's wrist and the captain actually whined. *He did like the idea.*

I glanced down and saw his cock was hard, Dante's hand wrapped around the base of it, and it was dripping. His body liked the idea, but of course none of us would do it unless he consented.

"All right," Gabriel said, his voice a little strangled. "If the doctor says it will help."

"I'm not actually a doctor," Oliver said. "But it will help." He slipped off the bed and returned quickly with some black silk rope.

"That's perfect," I said. Gently, carefully, I climbed over Gabriel to his other side, and between Oliver, Dante and myself we bound Gabriel's arms to his sides, creating a sort of ladder-like effect over his torso, the black rope standing out stark against his gently tanned and muscular chest.

My own arousal was intensely heightened. As much as I loved being dominated by Gabriel, and being bound, there was something so... well, taboo about doing this to him. And it thrilled me, making my own need greater to see him struggling a little as we tied the last knot and finding it secure.

"How does that feel, Captain?" Oliver asked, his voice smooth as satin. He punctuated this with a gentle nip on Gabriel's jaw.

"Actually very comfortable," Gabriel said.

"And is it hot?" I asked, wanting him to say it out loud. I tugged gently on the ropes on his wrist. He groaned softly.

"Yes," he said. "Now will someone please get on my cock?"

Oliver chuckled. "Even bound he can't give up control entirely."

"I'm fine with that," I said. I glanced at Dante, who had been stroking Gabriel with one hand. He tossed me the pot of coconut oil with his other.

"You go, Cedric," he said. "You're the one who's brought us all together, after all."

I caught the pot and pulled it open, smiling. "Thank you."

"I'll do it," Oliver said. He took the pot from me and twirled his finger in it. "Turn around and I'll prepare you, where Gabriel can easily watch." I did as Oliver said, and pushed my arse up, shuffling my knees apart and leaning back over Gabriel's chest. Oliver's finger instantly started to work me open.

Gabriel groaned again. "This is actually torture now."

"I think you're enjoying it even so," Oliver said.

I felt giddy, excited and aroused, and more than any of the rest, happy. My lovers were all together again, and we were trying something new, and all of it was so deliriously intoxicating.

"You love torture," I said, airily. "Don't act like you don't."

Gabriel huffed out a laugh. "Well, rest assured I will get my revenge for this."

"Can't wait." Then I couldn't talk anymore, because Oliver's fingers were inside me and Dante had drawn my head close enough to him to kiss and I lost myself in sensations. I breathed hard, nipping at Dante's lip and moaning.

Oliver's fingers stretched me open and then I felt his hands on my hips, gently tugging. Dante let me go and I climbed onto Gabriel's lap, letting warm and cool hands assist as I sank down onto his cock. Gabriel's moan was echoed by my own and I let myself sink down as fully as possible, rocking my hips infinitesimally to draw the feeling out as much as I could manage.

Behind me Dante moved in, close behind me, pressing his chest to mine and leaning in to kiss at my shoulder. I knew what he was angling for so I gently, so feather like gently it couldn't possibly hurt, drew my fingertips over Gabriel's chest.

"Do you want to see Dante biting me, Captain?" *It is technically his title. I usually use it when he's in charge, but it seems wrong to use a diminutive or a pet name for him even while he's the one tied up.*

"Yes," he replied instantly. His voice was hoarse and beautiful.

"Go on then, Dante," I said. I reached out to Oliver with my hand then, for all he had seemed content to watch the goings on, I wanted him involved. I hissed as Dante's fangs sank into my flesh, and Oliver moved closer, kissing me as I rose on my knees then sank back down again and again. I was full to bursting - Gabriel's hard, velvet smooth cock sliding in and out of me. Dante's fangs inside me, drawing my blood into him, life to life, and Oliver's tongue, tangling with mine and demanding my focus.

This was what it meant to be in my body. Not the curse, not the threat of losing control... being here with my lovers and feeling them. The specific scent of each of them blending into a heady fragrance I could get drunk on.

Oliver broke the kiss to give Gabriel the same treatment, and Gabriel's hips started to buck, pushing up into me with a sharpness that might have been bad for his wound, possibly, but mostly felt incredibly divine.

Dante's bite had me close to orgasming, but I wanted us all to achieve that in more or less the same moment, so I wrapped my fist tight around myself and gasped, trying to hold back the tide as I bounced on Gabriel's cock.

Then an even more arousing idea occurred to me.

"Dante, do you think... do you think..." I had to keep pausing to catch my breath. "Do you think you could get in there too?"

Oliver breathed out slowly. "Yes," Oliver said, sitting up straighter. "I want to watch that, see how it's done.

"I'll try," Dante said. "But only very slowly..."

He slicked himself with oil and then his fingers spread more of it around Gabriel's cock and my opening. His fingers pushed inside, testing if there was room, and stretching me further. It was a ridiculous suggestion I'd made when I was already trying to keep myself from orgasming but here we were. I was hardly going to take it back.

Oliver's hands were on me as well, helping, guiding my hips to slow, and to stay in position where Dante could work. Gabriel's cheeks were red and his eyes half closed, watching me. It occurred to me he was holding back his orgasm too, and I felt another flush of excitement through me. With my free hand I caressed his cheek and pushed my thumb into his mouth. Just because I could, and he couldn't stop me. He nipped my thumb gently and rolled his tongue over it. Again, I wondered at why I'd done this when I was already battling to keep my orgasm back.

Oliver's hands lifted me until just the tip of Gabriel's cock was still inside. Then I felt the press of Dante's cock as well. Both held together in Dante's fist as Oliver guided me to slide slowly down on both of them at once.

I'd never felt so full as I did then. Oliver's mouth claimed mine again, and he bit hard on my lower lip. Gabriel was sucking on my thumb and moaning, and Dante started to swear, quietly, in what I assumed was Romanian.

I don't know if I can survive this, I thought wildly. *This is true bliss, I could die now happily.* But that wasn't true at all, because if I could have this once then I could have it again.

I wrapped my arm around Oliver's shoulder and pulled him closer, loosening my hold on my cock so I could take his against mine and stroke us both.

I'm at the center of their universes right now. They are here with me, and together, whatever happens, we will get through it together. There's nothing too large to overcome if I have these men with me.

My orgasm wouldn't be denied any longer. I gasped a warning, although I hardly knew what noise I made, which wasn't just a whine or a moan.

In my hand, my cock throbbed against Oliver's and I started to come. Oliver gasped into my mouth, a sound almost like pain, as he came as well and my hand and Gabriel's stomach were coated with our mingled juices.

My squeezing and clenching around Gabriel and Dante had the same effect, spurring the both of them to fill me entirely, their cocks pressed together inside me, the hottest thing I'd ever experienced to that point.

CHAPTER 36

IN WHICH OUR STORY CONCLUDES FOR NOW

*B*etween Oliver and Dante's careful hands, we disentangled ourselves. It seemed most useful for me to keep my hips and arse still, so I busied my hands instead and freed Gabriel from his bindings.

Once everyone was free and clear, and a little cleaned up, I lowered myself onto the bed, tucking under Gabriel's arm. Oliver settled on the other side and Dante went behind me. There was a warm, golden glow to all of us and I felt my heart would burst with happiness.

"Fuck I love you," I said, surprising all of us. Oliver's eyes widened, but his startled grin softened into something more private and affectionate. He stroked his hand over my cheek.

"I love you too, Cedric," he said.

I swallowed, feeling my heart speed up again, but this time with nervousness. I tipped my head back and looked at Gabriel. "I love you, Captain."

Gabriel's cheeks pinked a little, again, and he stroked my hair with a hand that slightly trembled. "I know, Cedric. I..." he hesitated, long enough that I was about to tell him he didn't have to say anything in response, but then he shook his head. "I think I love you too, you unbelievable nightmare."

I closed my eyes because they'd teared up, and the lump in my throat was threatening to really choke me.

"Just let it happen," Dante murmured, pulling me closer into his chest, covering all of me with all of him. "We all love you, and you're allowed to feel whatever you're feeling. You're our precious treasure, and because of you, we all care for each other as well."

"That's true," Oliver's thumb rubbed my cheek so gently I truly felt like a fragile treasure. Like something worth taking care of.

"I don't know what the future holds," Gabriel said, as the tears flowed down my cheeks and dripped onto his chest. "But we will face it together."

"And just think," Oliver said, his tone more mischievous than before. "After tonight's successful experiment with two dicks in you at once, I have enough data to work out logistics for a triple penetration experiment perhaps."

I opened my mouth but it had gone dry and not a sound came out. My mind boggled, the idea of all three of them inside me at once? Was it even possible?

"Good work, Oliver. Excellent," Gabriel said. "You've found how to truly make Cedric speechless without a gag."

"Although the gag was very fun as well." Oliver kissed my shoulder and I sighed happily and closed my eyes.

In the morning we were all still tangled together in a happy puddle of pirates. I wondered, idly, as I woke up and looked between my lovers, if I was a pirate now. I expected I was, as I had been on the ship while they attacked others and stole their money. I definitely wasn't a hostage any more, which made me culpable in whatever crimes Gabriel led his crew into.

I found I didn't at all mind the thought of being a pirate, if it meant I got to stay here on the *Devil's Whore*.

By and by Oliver woke up, and he stirred enough that the others did too and we started the day with kisses.

Gabriel was declared well enough to resume light duties, Dante assisted him into clothes and then out to the deck where there were scattered cheers from the crew.

Oliver went back to his translation of the book and I attempted to help him. Mostly I sat and watched as his brow furrowed and smoothed and furrowed again.

"Got it," he said. "The cipher, I've cracked it. Now I just need to do some translating." He looked up at me and grinned with such pure pleasure I was pleased for him. I kissed him on the forehead.

"You're utterly adorable. I'll leave you to it, but let us know when you find something." I went out onto the deck and chatted with Kaito for the next hour or so.

Then Oliver emerged from the cabin with an expression less than thrilled. My stomach turned unpleasantly.

Once the four of us were back in the cabin, Oliver broke the news. He was seated at the desk with his notes to refer to. Gabriel was sitting on his bed and Dante and I leaned on the wall near the door.

"The book I got, it mentions a lot of what Cedric has told me about Nab and the Unknowable Way," he said. "I believe it might be a copy of the book Natalia Harrow is working from, or perhaps it's just a very similar book."

"That's great news," Gabriel said. "So why do you look like the news is bad?"

Oliver glanced at me, grimaced and sighed. "Because it is bad. Given what has happened with Cedric and the tattoo, it's very clear that what they have done is well, relentless or, perhaps progressive is the word. It doesn't matter if Harrow gets him back and does the damned ritual again, Cedric is being possessed by the tattoo, and... and by the thing it depicts."

"I am possessed?" I asked, and my voice sounded like it was from across the room.

"Yes, well, not exactly, it's in the process of possessing you."

I swayed on my feet and possibly would have fallen over but Dante caught my elbow.

"So, it's in the process," Gabriel said. "There must be a way to stop it."

"I think there is," Oliver said. "But the ritual seems to be so complicated, and it needs a number of people and all these things I've never heard of."

"What about the witches?" Dante asked. He helped me over to the bed beside Gabriel, but I sat apart from him. My skin chilled and goose pimpled again. The hopelessness of my situation swamped me. When I spoke again my voice sounded dry as paper.

"They scattered. I couldn't find Tanith… How can we gather them together when they've probably gone their own directions, they could be anywhere in the world."

"What does possession mean?" Dante asked. "In this context, what can we expect to happen to Cedric?"

I curled forward, bracing my forearms on my knees and my head on my arms. It was all too much, how was I supposed to handle this news?

My tattoo prickled unpleasantly and I tried to squash it down somehow.

Oliver's voice was dispassionate, a scientist relating data points. "He will lose himself to the thing itself. I won't say its name, the book says the name has power when spoken aloud. But Cedric's mind would yield to it, he would become the vessel of the thing and nothing more. And it would use its power to tear our reality apart."

My eyes were screwed closed, but I still saw black and silver stars before I passed out.

To be continued...

ACKNOWLEDGMENTS

A big thanks to Kitty and Liz. As ever, your feedback and your encouragement is so incredibly important to me.

My spouse is my number one everything. I couldn't write without their feedback and their faith in me. I love you so much.

I know it doesn't sound like much, but your review of this book actually does help. Amazon rewards reviews, and the more a book has, the more sales it gets. Please leave a review or a rating if you can!

The next installment of Cedric's story is coming soon.

Sign up for Drake's newsletter for updates on new releases

https://www.subscribepage.com/q4c4n0
Come join Drake's Crew reader's group to meet other fans and get exclusive content – maybe
you'll even get to name – or become! – a character in the next book
https://www.facebook.com/groups/1272511269588779/

Find Drake online:
Twitter: https://twitter.com/DrakeLamarque
Pinterest: https://www.pinterest.nz/drakelamarque/
Newsletter: https://www.subscribepage.com/q4c4n0
BookBub: https://www.bookbub.com/profile/drake-lamarque
Instagram: https://www.instagram.com/drakelamarque/

GENTLEMAN'S BOUNTY

BOOK 1 - KIDNAPPED BY THE GENTLEMAN

Buy now

Cedric has been kidnapped by pirates.

...they have no idea how much trouble they're in for.

Cedric was living his best life, partying in the colonies, bedding whomever he pleased and trusting that his parents' money and affluence would get him out of any unfortunate scrapes.

Until he was kidnapped by the fearsome pirate Lucifer, who planned to trade him for a hefty ransom. Unfortunately, he's not the only one after Cedric, and the strange secret society who have Cedric in their sights might just be more dangerous than Captain Lucifer.

Now Cedric is trapped on a pirate ship with a dashingly handsome captain, a quartermaster who won't stop staring at him and an overwhelming desire to find some fun, all while saving his hide from an unknown organisation who will stop at nothing to track him down.

GENTLEMAN'S BOUNTY

BOOK 2 - VAMPIRE'S INDULGENCE

Buy now

Unfortunately for Cedric Hale-Harrington, ignoring a curse doesn't make it go away. Especially when it's tattooed on his back.

After a close escape from the cult who want to sacrifice him, Cedric is happily aboard the Devil's Whore, staying close to his lovers, the dashing and dominant Captain Lucifer, the mysterious vampire Dante and his former tutor Oliver.

By rights, it should be a party all night, every night, But his dreams are getting steadily stranger, and he's brought something back from one of them. When bounty hunters start relentlessly pursuing the ship it looks like Cedric can't ignore the claim the cult has on him.

The Cult of the Unknowable Way draws ever closer and they aren't about to let him sail off into the sunset, not when they have a dark and potentially world-ending plan for him.

HIS PIRATICAL HAREM

BOOK ONE – CABIN BOY

Buy now

I've never been what I was supposed to be. Wealthy sons of Port Governors aren't supposed to be ejected from the British Navy after less than a year, they're not supposed to like pulp romances or daydream about the handsome heroes of the stories instead of the heroines.

When my Father issued me an order to marry a woman, I knew I had no choice but to make my own way in the world, and I found a berth on the first ship out of Jamaica.

I didn't mean to join a pirate ship, and I certainly didn't intend to find myself the cabin boy to an incredibly charming Pirate Captain. Or that I'd also be attracted to the mysterious First Mate, or that both of them would show me all sorts of unspeakable and salacious pleasures while on board. How can I choose just one of them when I want both?

In addition to confusion on board the ship, there's also enchanting genderfluid merfolk, a cat which seems to understand a lot more than it should, an unseasonable storm and a sea witch with a serious grudge... and with all these complications, I am definitely in over my head.

Come and meet the crew:

Gideon: an innocent with a lot of forbidden desires and a lot of love to give

Tate: a huge, muscular ship's captain with a sweet side

Ezra: a dominant and closed off first mate

Ora: a genderqueer, curious and affectionate merman

HIS PIRATICAL HAREM

BOOK TWO – FIRST MATE'S PET

Buy now

Things were looking good, until the ship's cat became a man...

I didn't mean to join a pirate ship, but now that I'm here, well. Life is pretty good. Between the sexy and intimidating Captain Tate, the mysterious First Mate, Ora the merfolk and now Zeb the ship's cat I'm well entertained.

Rumours abound that the Royal Navy are searching for me at my father's order, and between that, an eventful trip to Tortuga (the famed pirate town) and maintaining the relationships with the crew... I've certainly got my work cut out for me.

Meet the crew:

Gideon: a well bred young man who is discovering his forbidden desires aren't necessarily a problem at sea

Tate: the impressive Captain with a sweet side
Ezra: the controlling and alluring First Mate
Ora: a genderqueer, sweet and mystical merman
Zeb: a cat shifter, who's learning about being human

HIS PIRATICAL HAREM

BOOK THREE - MERFOLK'S MATE

Buy now

The British Navy caught up to the Grey Kelpie, and everything I'd built for my life has fallen apart.

Tate and Ezra are headed for the gallows. Ora has disappeared into an unwelcome sea and I have no idea what's become of the ship's cat...

It's up to me to save them, but I'm trapped on the Naval ship, the same as my lovers. If I'm to get us out of here, I'm going to have to use all my wits, and maybe a little magic?

Meet the crew:

Gideon: a well-bred young man discovering a new side of himself
   Tate: the sweet Captain with a dark past

Ezra: a dominating First Mate who's slowly finding his soft side

Ora: a mystical merfolk who understands more than the rest

Zeb: an affectionate cat shifter who knows what he wants

Content warning: some knife and blood play in one scene

HIS PIRATICAL HAREM

BOOK FOUR - CAPTAIN'S TREASURE

Buy now

I, Gideon Keene, have two big problems.

Two things, well, people, standing between me and my happiness.

One is a vengeful sea witch called Solomon, who has it in for me and my beloved Captain Tate.

The other is my father.

One has found us, the other is hounding us. It's time to take the battle to them, hold my head high and fight first one, then the other.

But how can a cabin boy, a ship's cat, a member of the merfolk and two pirates defeat the most powerful sea witch in the Caribbean? Tate betrayed him, badly, years ago and now his furious magic has drawn our ship to his blasted islands.

Assuming we survive, then take on the governor of Jamaica, who is determined to see me married to a nice girl and producing heirs?

This is going to take all the courage I have, all the magic I can summon to me, and the wits and understanding of each of my cherished lovers. Not one of us could do it alone, but maybe... just maybe, we can do it together.

ALSO PUBLISHED BY GREY KELPIE STUDIO

RIVAL PRINCES BY JAXON KNIGHT

Buy now

There are three golden rules for new recruits at Fairyland Theme Park:

1. No breaking character, even if you're dying of heat exhaustion
    2. Always give guests the most magical time
    3. No falling in love.

Nate's only been at work one day, and he's already broken all three.

Fast-tracked into a Prince role, Nate's at odds with Dash, the handsome not-so-charming prince who is supposed to be training him. Nate doesn't know how he ended up on Dash's bad side, but the broody prince sure is hot when he gets mad.

Dash has worked long and hard to play Prince Justice at Fairyland. Now, instead of focusing on his own performance, he is forced to train newbie Nate to be the perfect prince. Nate's annoying ease with the guests coupled with his charm and good looks could dethrone Dash from his number one spot ... so why does he secretly want to kiss him?

Fairyland heats up as sparks fly between the two rival princes. Will they get their fairytale romance before they're kicked out of Fairyland for good?

Find out in this standalone MM contemporary romance by Jaxon Knight, set in an amusement park where fairytales can come true.

ALSO PUBLISHED BY GREY KELPIE
STUDIO

MISCHIEF AND MAYHEM BY JAXON KNIGHT

Buy now

Mischief

Protecting royalty at Fairyland theme park seemed about as far from Afghanistan as Cody could get. But the hot new rollercoaster brings up some unexpected trouble - and not the kind of trouble he knows how to handle alone.

Mayhem

Dean loves running the Spaceship Mayhem roller coaster - he gets to meet new people every day! When he sees a handsome, troubled security guard repeatedly fail to ride it, he sees an opportunity to help. And maybe they can be more than friends?

Cody reluctantly accepts cute, boy-next-door Dean's help and sparks fly between them, but between mischief, mayhem and miscommunication, can they ever make a relationship work?

Mischief and Mayhem is a slow burn, opposites attract MM sweet romance featuring snark, foolishness, motorbikes, assumptions, the chicken door and a HEA

Buy now

The recipe is simple:
    Charlie cooks an amazing meal
    Charlie impresses heir to the theme park Max Jones
    Charlie gets a promotion and a dash of control over his
kitchen

But the perfect recipe becomes unpalatable with one wrong
ingredient and Max Jones is not behaving how Charlie
expected...

Max is meant to inherit the entire Fairyland theme park but he
just wants to party, have fun and bed as many people as possible.
That is, until he meets Charlie and falls for him so hard he can't
even finish the delicious meal.

Charlie doesn't have time for clubs or helicopter flights over the
city, but Max is accustomed to getting what he wants, and he
wants Charlie.

Featuring one part Billionaire, one part sensible chef, six cups of attraction, a generous dose of snark and a freshly prepared Happy Ever After.

ALSO PUBLISHED BY GREY KELPIE
STUDIO

THE GOOD, THE BAD AND THE DAD BY JAXON KNIGHT

Buy now

Haru is a single dad, a widower, doing his best to balance his career and raising his little girl, Minako. Thankfully Fairyland theme park is a haven for both of them. However, when both a prince and a pirate start courting Haru, his balancing act gets a lot harder...

Cillian plays a pirate at Fairyland theme park and he loves playing the roguish character in and out of work hours. The last thing he wants is to settle down with a guy with a kid, so can't he stop thinking about handsome single dad Haru. And why can't he stop looking at pictures of Prince Magnificence and his stupid symmetrical face? And why does he keep running into both of them?

Grayson feels he's found his home in the role of Prince Magnificence, but he's more likely to run from love than seek it out. Until he meets Haru, that is. Christmas is complicated by Grayson's role being featured in a special Christmas celebration. Not only that, but his feelings for Haru, and his possible rival

Cillian keep on growing. Maybe it's time to stop hiding who he really is?

The Good, the Bad and the Dad is a sweet MMM romance featuring a single father, a rogue and a trans prince with a heart of gold. No cheating, just the tentative first steps into polyamory.